A
Harlequin
Romance

OTHER
Harlequin Romances
by MARY BURCHELL

DO NOT GO, MY LOVE

by

MARY BURCHELL

HARLEQUIN BOOKS

TORONTO
WINNIPEG

Original hard cover edition published in 1964
by Mills & Boon Limited, 17-19 Foley Street,
London   W1A 1DR, England

© Mary Burchell 1964

Harlequin edition published February, 1972

SBN 373-01567-4

Reprinted August, 1972

Printed in Canada
1567

CHAPTER I

Penelope Masters raised her head from her homework (which required no effort at all, because her homework was not engaging more than a quarter of her attention anyway) and, observing that her family were ridiculously absorbed in their own affairs, she made the mournful statement:

"D'you know what I think? I think I'm getting paralysed."

This shocking announcement was received with stoical indifference. Though Margaret—whose sympathies could usually be relied upon—did ask absently:

"What makes you think that?"

"My fingers have gone all numb." Penelope waggled her right hand effectively and regarded it with interest.

"You've been leaning on your elbow too long," observed John, without looking up from his account books. "Try getting on with your homework. There's nothing like a little activity for curing pins and needles."

"This isn't pins and needles," stated Penelope with dignity. "Pins and needles *prickle*. This doesn't do anything."

"Just like you, you mean," retorted her brother, glancing up with a grin. "Well, what's the trouble?"

"It's arithmetic." Penelope was beside him in an instant. "I'm just not good at figures. But you're good at figures, aren't you, John? You're *wonderful* at figures, and so perhaps——"

"Stop fawning on me," said her brother good-humouredly. "What's this—a two or a three?"

"It's an eight." His little sister leaned heavily on his shoulder and breathed down the back of his neck. "It *began* as a two," added Penelope, whose meaning will be clear to all who are also not good at figures, "but I think it ought be an eight, after all."

"Too true it should be," agreed her brother. "What a disgusting mess you do make of your exercise books. Why they can't at least teach you kids to be neat I don't know. When I was at school——"

"Oh, not again!" groaned Penelope. "That's years ago anyway. Couldn't you just help me and not talk about what it was like before the Flood?"

"You've got your periods mixed," said her brother sternly. "We counted on our fingers and toes then." At which Penelope gave such an appreciative giggle that John smiled again and began to explain what she had somehow contrived to remain deaf to in class that morning.

"I believe Miss Pelham said something like that," murmured Penelope vaguely.

"I've no doubt she did, poor soul," said John with feeling. "And meanwhile, you and a couple of dozen other little horrors were looking out of the window and allowing your minds to go completely blank."

"Mine wasn't blank," declared Penelope virtuously. "I was thinking what a lovely day it was, and how nice it would be to be at the sea——"

"Who'd be a teacher!"

"——and I was also wondering what Dad was doing," finished Penelope pensively.

At these innocent words, Margaret glanced up from her sewing, Elinor—the beauty of the family—stopped polishing her nails and stared across at her little sister with widened grey eyes, and John allowed his pen suddenly to remain poised over the paper, motionless and rigid.

It was as though they were all caught in a moment of suspended animation, like people acting a tableau; even the cheerfully insensitive Penelope could not remain unaware that there was something strange in the atmosphere.

"What's the matter?" she inquired, glad of any

distraction from the boredom of sums. "Why are you all looking so funny?—like wax figures or something."

They all relaxed at that, but no one spoke for a moment, and then Penelope said again. "What's the matter? People *do* look out of the window and notice it's a lovely day, even in arithmetic lessons."

"And they also wonder what Dad is doing," remarked Elinor softly, and an angry little smile curled the corners of her beautiful mouth.

"Elinor——" There was a note of warning in Margaret's voice. But the other girl shrugged contemptuously and exclaimed, "We've got to tell her some time. Now is as good a time as any."

"Tell me what?" Penelope was immediately agog with curiosity.

Neither John nor Elinor seemed to feel equal to the task, so—characteristically—it was Margaret who braced herself to say:

"Something very unexpected has happened, Pen. We're just trying to get used to it ourselves and——"

"About Dad?"

"Yes."

"Is he dead?" inquired Penelope, with the simple ghoulishness of the very young.

"No, of course not!" For once, Margaret sounded faintly irritated, which showed the degree of tension she was feeling. "It's not—as bad—as that. He—it seems he got married last week and——"

"*Married?*" Penelope's voice ran up to an incredulous squeak. "Whatever for?"

The admirable brevity with which she had expressed all their inmost thoughts had the effect of making them catch their breath and then laugh. And, with the tension broken, Margaret said quite frankly:

"I don't know, Pen. I suppose that's what we're all asking ourselves. But then—the family life which has suited us all so well for so long may not really have been enough for Father. I don't know——" She broke off and sighed. "Maybe he felt he wanted someone more of his own age. Someone who would share his life in a way we can't. And even—run his household differently."

"You mean——" Penelope still sounded incredulous—"not have *you* run it any more?"

"If Father has married again, I can't imagine that his new wife won't want to run her own household," Margaret pointed out.

"But you've *always* run it!" cried Penelope indignantly. "And no one could have done it better."

This unsolicited testimonial touched Margaret more than she would have thought possible, and she bit her lip, though she managed to laugh slightly as she said, "Thank you, dear. But I haven't always run it, you know."

"Most of my life, anyway," retorted Penelope, who evidently thought poorly of any period before her own existence. "None of those early housekeepers really *counted*. You were always the centre of things. Even Dad always asked you about everything. Why should he need anyone else now? And who is it, anyway?"

"No one we know at all," stated Elinor, distinctly and distastefully. "A complete stranger. With some wretched little boy of her own——"

"Little boy?" Penelope brightened up considerably. "Oh, come, that's not so bad! What's his name and how old is he?"

"His name is Giles," Margaret explained, "and we don't know how old he is. Father speaks of—of her as being left a widow with a boy of twelve. But that may have been some years ago, Elinor."

"True." Elinor looked as though she found that thought even more distasteful. "I suppose he's sixteen or something ghastly like that by now."

"Why is sixteen ghastly?" Penelope wanted to know.

"Because all boys—not excepting John—become suddenly impossible to live with when they're about thirteen. And from then until they're nineteen or twenty they're simply the end," stated Elinor authoritatively. "Then, just as they're becoming possible to live with again, they go off and get married, and that's that."

Penelope gave a long, thoughtful stare at her brother, who was a great favourite of hers, and said, "You *are* over twenty, aren't you?"

"With quite a bit to spare," John assured her obligingly. "And perfectly ready to tan the objectionable Giles, if necessary."

"I think you're all rather mean," exclaimed Penelope. "I *like* the sound of Giles. And he may be only about fourteen, and that'll make him a nice companion for me. Besides——" then she stopped suddenly and clapped her hand to her dramatically open mouth—"Oh, I hadn't thought! We've got a *stepmother* now, haven't we?"

"We have," agreed the others, in a resigned chorus.

"Well—I don't know——" Penelope obviously re-examined the situation and began to smile slowly. "It's rather exciting, really, isn't it?" she said, disregarding the exasperated glances of her elders. "I mean—you go on for years, with nothing ever happening, and then, suddenly, all at once everything turns upside down and the whole—the whole pattern of life changes."

No one seemed specially delighted at having the pattern of life changed. But John said finally:

"It's Margaret who is going to feel it most, I'm afraid. At least Elinor and I go out to our respective jobs and——"

"But home is our background," interrupted Elinor angrily, "and we're used to coming back to it and—and *spreading* ourselves." She made an eloquent gesture with her really beautiful hands. "I don't want to come home and find a strange woman and some hobbledehoy youth cramping my style."

"Nor do I," agreed her brother fervently. "But for Margaret this place is her whole life."

"Oh, don't worry about me!" exclaimed Margaret— and then found herself colouring. For to no one—least of all her family—could she explain that this incredible new turn of events was not, in her own case, unmitigated disaster.

"There's no need to be beautifully self-sacrificing about it," said Elinor crossly. "Of course we worry about you. What are you going to do when you find there's no place for you in your own home, for goodness' sake?"

"Find a job, I suppose. Like you and John," Margaret replied lightly.

"What sort of a job?" inquired Penelope, who had a remarkable talent for asking the kind of question no one wants to answer.

"Oh, I—haven't thought about it much yet," Margaret conceded. "Perhaps something in the office at the Works, or——"

"Not in the office at the Works, if you take my advice," put in her brother dryly, and there was silence. For they all knew—even Penelope—that the one big family row within memory had been when John resolutely refused to go into his father's business.

Mr. Masters owned a small but highly successful iron foundry in one of those rather featureless towns which are dotted along the Tyne. Here it is possible to find, within quite a small area, the extreme ugliness of closely packed streets and the breathtaking beauty of surrounding countryside. And the question of whether one lives meanly or spaciously is largely decided by the part of the town in which one resides.

The Masters family lived on the outskirts of Cromburgh, in a pleasant, grey stone house, overlooking a magnificent stretch of country. There was nothing very beautiful about the architecture of the place, but it was solid and spacious, and built to withstand the keen winds which sweep across the Tyne Valley in winter time.

Here all of them had been born, and here their mother had died, less than a year after Penelope's appearance as very much the youngest of the family.

John and Elinor were twins and, though not at all alike in appearance, they shared that indefinable bond which exists very often between twins. It enabled them to guess at each other's reactions, share each other's sympathies and draw together in a curiously solid alliance at any moment of crisis.

Margaret, though two years younger, understood them and their characteristically eager and impatient reactions perfectly well, and this sometimes gave her the odd feeling of being much older than they were, so that she exercised towards them much the same sense of indulgent responsibility that she felt for her little schoolgirl sister.

People who had known her mother were apt to note Margaret's resemblance to her, and Aunt Martha—who descended upon them periodically for a critical visit of inspection, under the guise of social duty—never failed to remark that she could "see poor Cynthia in that second girl of yours, Robert". A vaguely censorious statement which always had the effect of making Margaret feel very much her father's child.

For though Margaret was, of the four of them, the least like the handsome, rather overbearing man who was their father, in an odd way she sympathized with him most.

Robert Masters was the kind of man for whom things usually went right—because he expected them to do so and put all the driving force of a confident, energetic nature behind his efforts. He had built up his own business from the ground and made it one of the most successful in the district. He had married the girl he wanted, in the teeth of considerable opposition from her family, and had eventually installed her in the kind of house no one had ever expected him to possess. In fact, for some years, everything had gone his way—just as he had expected it would.

But then the woman on whom nearly all his personal happiness depended had become tragically ill and, for the first time, he had found himself up against something over which he had no control. He was strangely helpless before impending, inevitable defeat, and when his wife died he was not only shattered by grief, but incredulous that this could happen to him.

Schoolgirl though she was at the time, Margaret had understood something of this and, from the first, she had tried her utmost to keep the family scene as unchanged as possible. Inevitably, from that time forward, the household had begun to revolve around her. And, by imperceptible degrees which she had hardly noticed herself, she had become as necessary to each one of them as the air they breathed.

Their father, meanwhile, threw himself more and more into his work, as though he felt that here at least his fate was in his own hands. Certainly no further check came to his life's plans until he made the incredible discovery that his only son had no wish whatever to go into the business.

With a frankness which Margaret could never have encompassed—but in which Elinor completely supported him—John explained, quietly but firmly, that he felt he would have more of a life of his own if his work lay outside the family circle. It was his way of saying that he did not intend to spend his life under the complete domination of his father.

If he had proposed to become an actor or a gipsy (the two were akin in his father's estimation) Mr. Masters could not have been more astounded or furious. Long and angry arguments followed, but John was not to be shaken. To his father's incredulous contempt, he wanted to be a market gardener. For John's love was growing things and the beauty of the earth. The exciting conflict of business and the dramatic fascination of white-hot furnace and molten metal held no attraction for him whatever.

"It's simply another way of life, Father," Margaret had said, when finally she felt bound to intervene. "And even the best of fathers can't live his children's lives for them. If your father had absolutely insisted on your growing fruit and flowers and vegetables, how would you have felt about it?"

Her father stared at her, his eyes puzzled and angry in his flushed, handsome face, and clearly what he would have felt about such a plan was unprintable.

"That's different," he countered. But, with mingled pity and relief, she saw the first signs of defeat in him. "This is a family business, and there's only John to carry it on."

"No, Father." Margaret spoke with diffidence but truth. "It is not a family business. It's *your* business. You built it up from nothing. It's your achievement and your life. If John had been the kind who wanted to continue in that line, it would have been wonderful—for both of you. But he isn't just a continuation of you. He is himself—and you know who would have been the first to say that?"

He was silent for almost a minute. Then he said reluctantly:

"Your mother."

She was dreadfully sorry for him. And, if he had been another type of man, she would probably have gone to him and put her arms round him. But he would have been irritated—perhaps even embarrassed—by any show of feeling which took into account the fact that he had been defeated. So she just left him to assimilate the undeniable truth of what she had said.

A day or two later, he announced that if John was determined to spoil his own life, he supposed he had some sort of absurd right to do so. After which he bought his son a modest piece of land, lent him a small amount of capital, and waited for him to make an ignominious failure.

But John was not his father's son for nothing. Having struggled through a hard winter, and the kind of summer which is practically indistinguishable from a mildish winter, John contrived, with immense exertions, to break even.

On the day that he began to pay back his father's loan,

a sort of reluctant respect crept into Mr. Masters' manner. And, although he and John would never enjoy that close, intimate relationship which exists between many fathers and sons, they tolerated each other with a certain degree of good humour and mutual respect.

About his daughters' futures Mr. Masters had been much less difficult. After all, no one would expect anything as utterly lovely and feminine as Elinor to concern herself with an iron foundry. On the contrary, with her gorgeous red-gold hair, perfect complexion and clear, brilliant grey eyes which she inherited from her father, she had found little difficulty in securing employment in the dress department of the most exclusive store in Newcastle. Here she had passed rapidly through the stages of model girl and saleswoman, and was already the youngest assistant buyer in the firm.

With such examples of enterprise and determination before her, Margaret had gone through a short period of feeling it was rather tame of her just to stay at home and keep house. But, from the youthful, pliant and sometimes oddly defenceless Penelope to the dictatorial, demanding and occasionally extravagantly appreciative Mr. Masters, they all had their special need of her.

At first, Margaret thought that perhaps she was flattering herself in this respect. But the unspeakable and concerted dismay with which they greeted even a tentative suggestion that perhaps she too should earn her own living was enough to convince her where her real work in life lay.

"Don't be ridiculous!" her father had said in alarm and surprise. "You *do* earn you own living—here. What do you want—a larger allowance?"

And, since careless generosity was one of his outstanding characteristics, he promptly and substantially increased her allowance—under slight protest from Margaret—and this was the sole result of her little gesture for freedom and independence.

Not that Margaret minded. She loved her life and she

loved her home. And until she met Paul Freemantle she could not imagine that she would ever be discontented with her lot.

She had met him at the Northern Charities Ball in Newcastle, and at first she had been afraid that he was not interested in her. Then she was afraid that he might become too much so. For one could not expect anyone as quick and forceful and smilingly impatient as Paul to understand that her every major action was decided on the basis of family claims.

He drove out from town to see her quite often—usually during the daytime, so that the family had no reason to realize how often she saw him—and, handsome and dynamic, he tried to sweep her off her feet.

"Of course there's a way out! There always is," he had protested impatiently, when she answered his first declaration of love with the insistence that there was no immediate prospect of her being free. "What's so vital about your place in the family, anyway? John and Elinor are old enough to manage their own affairs, and a good housekeeper could run this place as easily as you."

"There's Penelope——" she began. But Paul had caught that up immediately.

"And a more self-sufficient kid I never clapped eyes on," he declared. "She's got enough self-assurance to sink a battleship. A real chip off the old block, if ever there was one. If she and your father can't manage without you, I don't know what you're talking about."

"They need me in a dozen subtle, inexplicable ways," she protested. "They——"

"I need you too!" he cut in angrily. "In more than a dozen ways, and not so subtly either." And at that point he pulled her against him and kissed her hard, in a way that made strange little quivers of excitement run up and down her. "Stop prevaricating, Meg. Do you love me or——"

"I love you," she said, with a simplicity which made

him gentler, and when he took her in his arms and kissed her more tenderly it was even more difficult to remember just what the family claims were.

"Paul, if you'd be patient——"

"I'm not a patient man," he told her grimly.

"No, I know. And I haven't the right to ask you to wait an indefinite period. I realize that. But Penny is so terribly young, and far more dependent on me than you can guess. And the other two, though warm and loving, have tremendously explosive temperaments. In a way, the peace with Father is a bit precarious, and until John is established——"

"If you think we can wait until John makes his fortune, Elinor marries one of her half-dozen admirers and Penelope grows up, you haven't got me aright, Meg," Paul said quickly. "Think again, darling."

She thought again. She thought of the wonderful future she could have with Paul, whose life as foreign correspondent for a chain of provincial newspapers took him to the most fascinating places. He constantly enthralled her by descriptions of dawn over the Alps, evening stillness on the Italian Lakes, unbelievable colour in the bazaars of the Near East. And, though she could hardly expect to accompany him to all these places, compared with her restricted life in Cromburgh, the world would be hers.

But then—what would the family do?

"Paul," she said, "you'll have to give me at least the time to think out my own personal solution. I'll try not to strain your patience too far. But I can't just spring this on them without some sort of preparation."

So, reluctantly, he had promised to give her a little time.

And then, two days later, the utterly unexpected happened. Her father—who had never been ill in his life, so far as she could remember—suddenly and terrifyingly developed double pneumonia. What had seemed nothing but an obstinately neglected cough flared into crisis.

Understandably, he was not a good patient and bitterly

resented the weakness and enforced idleness of many weeks. But, to a degree that was almost pathetic, he depended on his second daughter for nearly everything, and she devoted herself untiringly to his care.

When it was finally broken to him by his doctor that he had been undermining a fine constitution with systematic overwork for years and was now showing signs of heart weakness, he, accepted the warnings with unexpected docility and agreed to take a long holiday.

During the anxious weeks of his illness, Margaret had perforce seen little of Paul, in spite of some insistent telephone calls. And, on the one occasion on which they contrived to meet for any length of time, they came so near to quarrelling that she, as well as he, said things which would take a lot of forgetting and forgiving.

"If you really loved me," he had cried angrily, "you wouldn't for ever put your family before me."

"And if *you* really loved *me*," she retorted angrily, "you'd understand my predicament and show a little sympathy and understanding."

They made it up, in a fashion, before he left her. But the next time he telephoned it was to tell her that he had to go abroad on a fairly lengthy assignment, and he ended by saying, "By the time I come back, Meg, I hope you'll have decided who is to come first in your life."

His absence had been agonizing enough for her to know she *must* find a solution. But, in her wildest moments, she had not expected to have a ready-made one presented to her.

To be sure, she thought, as she looked round now on her brother and her sisters, it could not be rated an ideal solution. No one was looking specially happy about the immediate prospect. But the simple fact was that, of his own free will, her father had set someone else in her place. Without a single qualm of conscience, she not only could, but should, make her life elsewhere.

"When are we to expect them?" inquired Penelope, breaking the long silence which had settled on them all after John's remark about the inadvisability of Margaret's seeking work in her father's office.

"Friday," said Margaret, picking up a letter from the table beside her. "Which is the day after tomorrow. So we'd all better get used to the idea as quickly as possible and decide to put a good face on things. After all, in spite of protests, Father has allowed us all to live our own lives——" For a moment her glance deliberately met John's. "The least we can do is to let him live his."

"But at *his* age——" murmured Elinor protestingly.

"Father is a vigorous man in his early fifties," Margaret retorted firmly.

"How early?" inquired Penelope inquisitively, but no one took any notice of that.

"And if he and Eileen——"

"Who's Eileen?" interrupted Penelope again.

"The woman he's married, you goose," exclaimed Elinor impatiently. "Let Margaret finish her little homily." And again she curled her lip in that scornful but attractive manner.

"It's not a homily!" Margaret flushed and laughed. "I'm only trying to be reasonable and—and fairly just about this. For good or ill, Father's taken this step—which he's perfectly entitled to take—and we've just got to accept it. For all we know, *he* may be having his worried moments and be feeling rather jumpy about presenting his new wife to us."

"Father never felt jumpy in his life," Elinor declared confidently. "He's the one who makes the others jump."

And, on this uncomfortably correct assessment of the case, the family discussion ended for the moment.

Penelope, her homework perfunctorily completed, was allowed half an hour with her bosom friend from next door, a spectacled child called Dorothy Emms, whose natural ability to be top of the class was as naught in the eyes of her contemporaries beside the fact that she could wiggle her ears.

Elinor was collected by the latest of her admirers, in a

rakish-looking sports car, and John went off on some affairs of his own. So that Margaret was left to her own devices, and she took this opportunity to go out into the kitchen and break the news of the impending change to Gloria, their reasonably devoted maid.

In spite of her name, and a hair-dressing vaguely reminiscent of Vesuvius in eruption, Gloria was a good, hard-working girl. And, since she was romantic by temperament, the very word "wedding" made her eyes glisten.

"Well, I suppose even the old can do with a bit of romance some time, Miss Margaret," was her tolerant comment on this upheaval in the household. "But who'd have thought it of the master?"

Who indeed? reflected Margaret. But aloud she explained that, under the new régime, Gloria would be answerable to a new employer and that a few readjustments might have to be made.

"Oh, I'll soon get her used to my ways, I expect," said Gloria kindly. And, since she obviously meant no offence in this reversal of the natural order of things, Margaret wisely decided to leave it to time and Gloria's natural good-humour to accomplish whatever changes were required.

When Friday came, Margaret found herself without the support of either her brother or her elder sister. John quite unavoidably had to attend to a large consignment of vegetables required for the Saturday market, and Elinor *said* she had to work late at the shop. But she had flickered her long lashes as she made this statement, and Margaret knew she was always being less than ingenuous when she did that. In all probability, she had been asked to stay late and, instead of trying to make a rearrangement, had thankfully accepted this chance of absenting herself from the awkward scene of arrival.

Penelope at least was willing to play her part. She rushed home from school at top speed, accompanied by an excessively curious Dorothy Emms, who was also quite obviously ready to join the reception committee if allowed.

"Can Dorothy stay too?" inquired Penelope, while Dorothy gazed hopefully at Margaret through her spectacles and remarked, "I've never seen a stepmother."

"Not this afternoon." Margaret was quite equal to this sort of appeal, having had to deal with it, in varied forms, many a time before. "We'll be pleased to see you later on, Dorothy. But we're having just a family gathering at first, and I expect your mother is waiting tea for you already."

"She wouldn't mind waiting a bit longer," declared the accommodating Dorothy. But Margaret shepherded her kindly but firmly towards the door, and Dorothy finally took her departure with the air of one who had made a good try, but bore no one any ill-will because of failure.

"Are you nervous?" Penelope asked, as Margaret moved about the room, setting one or two things unnecessarily to rights.

"No! No, not at all," Margaret asserted less than truthfully.

And then there was the sound of a car arriving, and, looking from the window, Margaret saw her father— bronzed and remarkably youthful-looking—helping a beautifully dressed woman from the car, with a good deal more care and attention than he was in the habit of lavishing on any of his daughters.

She was of medium height and slightly built and, though hatless, looked incredibly smart, from the beautifully burnished copper of her hair (superbly styled) to the light, elegant shoes on her slender feet. Altogether there was an air about her which made her a vaguely unreal figure in the down-to-earth setting of Cromburgh.

With her attention riveted upon this unbelievable addition to the household, Margaret hardly even noticed that a tall, good-looking young man followed her father and her new stepmother up the garden path. If she took him in at all, it was merely as the man who was carrying the luggage.

She ran out and flung open the front door, with as convincing an air of welcome as she could achieve, to find herself being greeted with real affection by her father and a soft bump of the cheek and a murmured, "Dear Margaret," by his companion. Then Eileen—for so one was going to have to call her, presumably—glanced casually over her shoulder and added :

"This is my son, Giles."

"G—Giles!" stammered Margaret. "But I thought ——"

She managed to bite back what she had thought. But Penelope, devoid of any such polite inhibitions, exclaimed incredulously :

"But we thought you were a little boy! Or at least a *schoolboy*."

"I've been both in my time," the young man assured her. "But the years change us all, you know."

"Don't tease her." His mother smiled sweetly—past Penelope rather than at her, which gave the odd impression of her not thinking it worth while to focus her full attention on the little girl. "She just can't imagine that I could be the mother of a great big fellow like you."

"Oh, yes I can," said Penelope, with an unpromisingly aggressive note in her voice. But, before she could enlarge on that, Margaret ushered them all into the large comfortable dining-room, where an excellent tea was already set out on the table.

"It's a charming house." Eileen looked round with gracious approval. "Full of possibilities, Robert. I shall *adore* doing it over." And then, before Penelope could close the mouth she had opened in resentful astonishment, she glanced at the table, shuddered very slightly and murmured, "Oh dear, what a *lot* of food."

"We all have good appetites in this house," stated Penelope. "My best friend Dorothy, who lives next door, says——"

But the views of her best friend Dorothy who lived next door were cutting no ice with anyone. For Mr. Masters was already fussing over his new wife, installing her comfortably in the chair which had always been regarded as Margaret's, and inquiring about her every wish, with a devoted attention which faintly embarrassed Margaret.

It was Giles who, quite unexpectedly, said obligingly:

"Tell *me* about Dorothy. Is she the same age as you?"

"She's a month younger. But she's top of the class," explained Penelope, delighted to talk about herself and her associates. "And she can wiggle her ears."

"Astonishing," said Giles gravely. "Can she raise one eyebrow without the other?"

"N—no, I don't think so. Can you?" Penelope asked.

"Certainly," said Giles, and did so.

"Goodness!" Penelope was visibly impressed. "It makes you look terribly—terribly——"

"Quizzical?" he suggested.

"Well, I don't know what that means. But it makes you look *interesting*," Penelope said.

"Giles, stop teasing that child and pulling faces at her," exclaimed Eileen a little fretfully. And it occurred to Margaret that she was not altogether pleased to have too much attention directed away from herself.

"You—you'd like some tea, I expect?" Margaret, who was by nature the most hospitable of creatures, suddenly found herself oddly diffident about what she had to offer.

"Just a cup of tea, dear. China, if possible. And no milk—only a slice of lemon. No, nothing to eat, thank you. I'm a little fatigued with the journey."

She didn't *look* fatigued. She looked absolutely blooming, Margaret thought. But charitably telling herself, in the words of the district, that perhaps "her looks didn't pity her", Margaret gave her new stepmother a sympathetic smile and hurried out into the kitchen, to forestall Gloria's undoubted intention of producing what she herself called "a good pot of tea with some *body* to it".

It was not an easy meal. With complete strangers one can talk only of surface things. Yet with people who have some claim to being part of one's family, one has to try to do better than that. Eileen did not make things any easier by her subtle way of implying—though without once raising her voice or making any real complaint—that everything was just a little open to criticism.

Indeed, the only real enthusiasm she displayed was when she spoke—as she did more than once—of the alterations she proposed to make in the house and the way it was at present run. All of this Mr. Masters seemed to find perfectly natural and understandable, Margaret noticed, and it was only with the greatest difficulty that she could repress her own indignation and resentment.

Naturally, one would expect the new Mrs. Masters to want to make her own rearrangements. But need the two of them talk so much as though the present régime and the present family were to be elbowed aside, as having little value and few claims?

"After all, *we* have been Father's family for over twenty years," thought Margaret indignantly. "Are we to be entirely superseded?"

While she pursued these angry reflections, she somehow also managed to converse rather formally with Giles —whose surname, Penelope had discovered without loss of time, was Ormby. He had nothing whatever of his mother's calculated sweetness of manner. Indeed, most of his answers were abrupt and economical. But his unusually attractive speaking voice did something to soften the impact of his curt wording.

Apart from his admired ability to raise one eyebrow without the other, he had fine dark eyes and good bone-structure to his face. But the mouth and chin were firm— even obstinate, Margaret noted—and once or twice she had the impression that he found her amusing when she had not intended to be.

By the time Elinor put in an appearance, Margaret was beginning to feel the strain—and she only hoped he was too, she thought, with less than her usual degree of good-humour.

"Ah, the beauty of the family, I see," commented Eileen as she greeted the newcomer. But, oddly enough, the remark conveyed less of a compliment to Elinor than disparagement of what she had already seen, one felt.

"That's a matter of opinion," Elinor retorted coolly, for—tiresome and impatient though she could be within the bosom of her own family—she allowed no outsider to disparage any member of it. "Some people think Margaret's eyes and complexion the best features in the family. And even Pen has her admirers."

"Have I?" said Penelope, looking very much astonished. But, at a quelling look from her elder sister, she took the point and, smirking complacently, she added, "Well, perhaps I have."

This seemed to amuse Giles not a little and, at the sound of his laugh, Elinor turned and looked at him.

"Hello—who are you?" she inquired.

Explanations were once more offered and Elinor bestowed upon him the slow, dawning smile which she had found remarkably effective in her young life up to now.

"A much more interesting addition to the family than a scrubby schoolboy," she remarked. "That is—if you *are* an addition to the family. Shall we be seeing much of you?—or are you here merely to see your mother safely established?"

It was a question which Margaret had been longing to ask, and she turned and looked full at him as he replied:

"I'm going to live here in Cromburgh, if that's what you mean. As for living here in the house——"

"Darling, we don't need to go over all that again, do we?" interrupted his mother plaintively. "Of course my home is your home—wherever it may be."

The expression of this charming sentiment had the affect of arresting all further conversation immediately. And it was Penelope who finally asked doubtfully:

"But what will you *do* here? I mean—what's your work, exactly?"

"I'm in the same line as your father."

He stated the fact with the directness and economy of words that he had used in all his answers. But, looking at him, Margaret saw the line of his mouth tighten and she had the idea that either he was preparing to be difficult or—much more improbably—that he was feeling nervous.

"What a—coincidence." That was Elinor, suddenly withdrawn and no longer smiling.

"Not entirely." Mr. Masters cut across the conversation with characteristic and aggressive clarity. "I'm taking Giles into the business. I need a younger man. It's all been getting too much for me. He'll be coming in first as a partner and later as my successor."

"Over the heads of all of us—and John?" Unexpectedly, it was Margaret who, white with anger and dismay, flung the leading question at her father.

"John has made it abundantly clear that he has no interest in the business," retorted Mr. Masters curtly.

"But he's *young*, Father! Not even fully established in his own line. People change their minds as they get older. To do this without even consulting him——"

"I'm not in the habit of consulting people who change their minds. I have no time for them," her father interrupted dryly. "I've found less than no support for my life's work in my own family. It's a great consolation to me that I should find enthusiastic interest and support in —my new family." He smiled and patted Eileen's shoulder. "Things could hardly have arranged themselves more fortunately."

"That, of course," said Giles, speaking for the first time, "is, as Elinor put it earlier, a matter of opinion. I'm not expecting everyone to fall on my neck with cries of welcome——"

"Well, that's something!" remarked Margaret, with crude, schoolgirlish sarcasm more suited to Penelope than herself.

"——But I hope you'll reserve judgement until——"

"There's no need for lengthy explanations," cut in Mr. Masters shortly. "The girls never have understood much about the business, and they won't start now. There are bound to be a few hard thoughts at first. But we'll shake down all right. We'll shake down."

Nobody looked at all like shaking down at that moment. But perhaps everyone sensed that further discussion could only result in the kind of statements and counter-statements that could never be unsaid. So, with a tremendous effort, Margaret turned, with courtesy if not cordiality, to her stepmother and said:

"Perhaps you'd like me to show you your room—and the rest of the house?"

"Lovely, dear!" Eileen looked so completely forgiving that Margaret was hard put to it not to slap her. Instead, however, she accompanied her upstairs and, having helped her to complete a tour of inspection, left her in contented possession of the best room in the house, while she herself fled to her own bedroom.

"It's outrageous!" Margaret walked up and down, talking to herself in angry whispers. "I know John thinks he has no interest in the firm—and of course we girls haven't any *practical* interest in it. But if Father needed an assistant—and he well may—he should have *employed* one. He can't just hand over the—the family birthright to a stranger."

It occurred to her that perhaps her wording was becoming a little melodramatic and unreasonable. But, when she thought of the invasion that had just taken place, it was difficult not to panic angrily at this fresh indication of conquest.

"There won't be room for any of us," she thought, anxiety sharpening her judgement. "Eileen's like one of those attractive toy dogs that get up beside you on the sofa and never rest until they've edged you off. If only John makes a success in his chosen way of life—that will be something! And Elinor—I suppose Elinor will always make a place for herself. With a first-class job and an interesting circle of friends in Newcastle, she wouldn't be unhappy. And anyway, she's the kind to marry early. Which leaves only Pen——"

She thought for a little while about her younger sister, with tenderness and some amusement. For she realized that, of them all, Penelope was probably the one who would settle down with the interlopers. Already she was on excellent terms with Giles. Before long, Margaret reflected with a small pale smile, *he* would be doing her homework.

And then, if all this settled itself—whether they liked the form of the solution or not—she herself would be free. Free of the dear but inescapable bonds which had held her so long. Free to tell Paul that she could marry him whenever he liked.

"If it hadn't been done in such an arbitrary and unfair way, I suppose I might be almost grateful to those two," she thought reluctantly. And at least, because of Paul, she was not going to have to share the house with Eileen!

"Think what that would have meant!" she admonished herself grimly. "And be thankful for Paul."

Oh, she *was* thankful for Paul! Inexpressibly, rapturously thankful. For the first time for weeks—no, for the first time since she had known him—she could think of him freely, without guilty restrictions. She could take her happiness with both hands and feel remorseful about no one.

She was smiling as she went downstairs again—once more the calm, well-balanced, sweet-tempered girl who had been the centre of the Masters household for so long. And when she came into the large, pleasant drawing-room and found only Giles Ormby there, she experienced no more than a twinge of unfriendly resentment at his presence.

He was standing by the window, looking out over the garden to the country beyond. And, with an air of determining to be civilized in a rather explosive situation, he remarked formally:

"What very beautiful country you have round here."

"Yes. We're lucky to have this view." She spoke a little stiffly, for it was still difficult not to regard him as a man who had wormed his way shamefully far into her father's favour. But she came over to stand beside him and point out where the flash of light on moving water disclosed the unspoiled reaches of the upper Tyne, long before it became the great waterway for shipping and commerce.

"Few people know how lovely this part of the Valley can be," she said.

"It's pleasant to see it for oneself," he agreed. "But I've heard its praises sung by someone else. I ran into an acquaintance from here at my club last week. A newspaperman from Newcastle, called Paul Freemantle. A very brilliant fellow, I believe."

"Paul—Freemantle?" She smiled very slightly. "And you told him you were coming to Cromburgh?"

"I didn't specify Cromburgh, only the Tyne Valley. As a matter of fact, he was rather too full of his own affairs to listen much to mine." Giles smiled slightly in his turn. "He'd just got engaged. Rather a whirlwind affair, I gathered. Some girl up here had kept him dangling for ages, unable to make up her mind—and then this other business had hit him like an atom bomb. Well——" he shrugged and laughed—"I suppose that's the way these things happen."

"Yes," said Margaret slowly, with the odd conviction that she could actually hear her world crashing around her, "I suppose that's the way these things happen."

CHAPTER II

Giles Ormby continued to look out of the window and, for nearly a minute, there was silence. Then he suddenly seemed to become aware of the fact that the girl in the room behind him was unnaturally still. He turned quickly and asked:

"Is something the matter?"

"No—nothing." With an effort Margaret roused herself from the deadly feeling of numbness which had come upon her.

"But you look so pale and—stricken, somehow. There must be something wrong. Something more than the general family situation, I mean," he added, as though recalling that quite a lot was wrong in that respect.

She shook her head wordlessly. But he obviously remained unconvinced. For he frowned, as though in an effort to remember, and went on:

"Was it something I said? And yet—no, we were only talking about the countryside, and my friend Paul Freemantle, and——" He stopped suddenly, and she saw something like consternation dawning on his expressive face. "Lord," he said softly, "do you—know Paul Freemantle?"

"Yes."

For all she tried, she could add nothing to that monosyllable. But the one word must have been revealing enough, because he said slowly:

"I'm terribly sorry. You're the girl he—ditched, of course?"

"You could put it that way," she agreed, and she rubbed her hands nervously together, as though she had suddenly discovered that they were cold. "But perhaps I was to blame too. Perhaps, as you put it, I—kept him dangling too long."

"Nonsense!" He repudiated that idea with emphasis.
"You couldn't. You're just not that sort."

"How do you know what sort I am?" she retorted
wearily.

"Well, I don't know in detail, of course." He seemed
slightly taken aback himself to find how authoritatively
he had pronounced upon her. "But I'm quite certain
you're not the kind of girl to keep a man on tenterhooks
just for the fun of it—just for nothing."

"It wasn't for nothing. At least——" she sighed impatiently—"it seemed terribly important at the time. I
didn't feel I could leave the family. It was as simple as
that. I've always managed everything for them, and I felt
I simply must work out some new pattern before I left
them. Then Father was ill, and I hardly had time even
to see Paul. It must have been maddening for him—I do
see that. And—he's not a patient man."

She remembered his saying that himself. And the way
he had kissed her and pleaded with her when he made the
admission. And suddenly there were tears in her eyes and
it was difficult to blink them away and look as though
nothing much was the matter.

"Do the others know?" he asked, after a moment.

"Oh, no! Nobody has any idea. Except you," she
added, a little wonderingly, because it seemed incredible
that this man—a stranger, and an unwanted stranger at
that—should know more about her than her own family.

"Don't worry," he said curtly, "I shall keep it to myself. I'm sorry I found out so clumsily. I don't seem to be
making a specially good start in this household, do
I?"

"It's not your fault." She made a visible effort to be
fair. "I mean—it's not your fault that you should be the
one to—to tell me about Paul. It just happened that way.
It could have been—anyone. And I suppose it was better
that I should hear now, rather than later. After I'd had
time to—to make plans for the future, I mean."

He thrust his hands into his pockets and stared at the

floor, which gave her time to wipe away a couple of tears surreptitiously. Then he said, "I suppose you were working out the future in terms of—marrying him?"

"At least I was not contemplating staying on here," she agreed shortly.

"And now you'll have to?"

"Oh, I don't know—I don't know," she cried rather wildly. Then, calming herself with another effort, she said more quietly, "I'll think of something, but I don't know what at the moment. It's all so—unexpected." She made a helpless little gesture with her hands, and he was silent, until she asked, as though she simply could not help it, "Have you—seen her?"

"Yes," he admitted, "I've seen her. In fact, I was introduced to her. Her name is Hester Graham and she's——"

"Hester Graham? But I *know* her!" cried Margaret, in sudden consternation. "By sight, I mean. Her family live further up the Valley. She's small and fair and—and very lively, isn't she?"

"That describes her—yes." He seemed reluctant to go on with the subject, but she had to know more.

"But I imagined that he met her first in London! You said it was all quite sudden. A whirlwind romance."

"Paul's words, not mine," he retorted, obviously taking no responsibility for the description.

"But then he must have known her before. At least——" she pushed back her hair distractedly. "No, of course—he might just have met her in London, and their coming from the same district gave them something in common, and then——"

"Stop tormenting yourself," he interrupted impatiently. "What do the details matter?"

"Of course they matter!" She turned on him almost violently. And then said, "Oh, I'm sorry. But—don't you see?—this matters terribly. Because they'll be coming back here—they'll be around in the neighbourhood. If it had all happened in London, and she was someone

I didn't know and need never see, I could just have borne it. But—this!"

"You'll have to bear this too," he pointed out, though with not unkindly realism. "And because you're a brave girl, you'll carry it off all right. If I can, I'll help you."

"You?" She recoiled from him, suddenly hating the fact that he knew so much about her intimate self. "I don't want your help, thank you. And what could you do, anyway?"

"I don't know, exactly," he confessed. "Save your pride on some occasion by playing the part of a fresh admirer, or something like that, I suppose."

"I can't imagine that being necessary," she said coldly.

"You're probably right." Immediately, he was as withdrawn as she. And then Penelope came bustling into the room, and their conversation was over.

"Guess what——" Penelope was full of importance.

"What?" inquired Giles obligingly.

"Elinor says she's going to have a flat of her own in Newcastle. She says she doesn't intend to live here any longer, and that it isn't worth while to go in and out to town every day if her home is all spoiled when she gets back to it."

"Hush!" said Margaret mechanically, but too late. While Giles smiled in that cool, scornful way of his, and observed, with a dangerous glint in his eyes :

"You don't seem to be anxious to come to any sort of terms, as a family, do you? Instant success or nothing with you, and I'm afraid my mother and I haven't made much of a hit."

"You have. Not her," stated Penelope, with splendid partiality if poor grammar.

"Thanks," was the dry reply. "But, as a dutiful son, I can scarcely accept that with acclamation."

"Oh, stop talking nonsense, the two of you," exclaimed Margaret, very nearly at the end of her self-control. "Elinor loves striking attitudes, and usually doesn't mean more than half of what she says. That's the way people are in a family. You probably aren't used to this sort of thing, being an only son. But if you're going to live here——"

"*Are* you going to live here?" interrupted Penelope, with an inquiring look at Giles.

"I don't think so," he said slowly.

"Your mother says you are."

"My mother doesn't know everything about me," he retorted.

"No, I don't expect she does," agreed Penelope, and for some reason this struck her as extremely funny. She burst into uninhibited laughter and, after a moment, Giles grinned, though reluctantly.

"I don't know what's so funny about that," he began.

"Except that I think she would *like* to know everything about you," replied Penelope, with the awful sagacity of the young. "And I bet you really have a Secret Life."

"Oh, come," he protested, "I'm not a specially dark horse, I assure you. It's just that——" he paused and looked surprised at finding himself on the verge of explaining the rather delicate relationship with his mother to a little girl.

It was Margaret—more versed in the art of side-tracking Penelope—who came to his rescue, by asking:

"Where are all the others? It must be nearly dinner time."

"Eileen's in her room. Elinor's sort of raging round the garden on her own. And Dad and John are having a row in the study," replied Penelope with great exactness.

"Having——?" Margaret looked suddenly apprehensive. "How do you know they're having a row?"

"Because they're both talking very loudly, and the smoke's pretty well coming out under the door," replied Penelope with a nice degree of imagery.

"Oh—dear!" Margaret put her hand to her head for a moment, for she had just realized it was aching. "They mustn't do that! It's so bad for Father—and for John too, in a way. I'd better——"

She would have made for the door, but Giles's hand on her arm suddenly arrested her.

"No—not you," he said, quietly but with authority. "You've had enough for one evening. I'll go."

"You?" She looked at him in astonishment. "But it's a *family* matter. You can't interfere."

"Why not? I suppose I'm the cause of the row," he replied coolly. "And everyone seems to be jumping to pretty hasty conclusions about my position around here. Before your father and your brother get at each other's throats, I'd better go and make a few points clear."

And, putting her aside, he went out of the room, leaving Margaret to stare after him in perplexity. There was silence for a moment. Then Penelope said brightly:

"He's rather nice, isn't he?"

"I—don't know——" Margaret began, very truly. But, before she could define her views further, Elinor came in from the garden, looking so pale, obstinate and unsmiling that Margaret was moved to ask anxiously:

"What's this about your going off to Newcastle and having a flat of your own, Elinor?"

"I can't see anything else for it!" Elinor walked angrily up and down the room, which made connected conversation difficult but gave her some splendid opportunities for dramatic gesture. "I just couldn't remain under the same roof with those two."

"Isn't it a little early to decide?" Margaret suggested mildly. While Penelope, bursting with the latest news, said:

"Giles probably doesn't intend to live here anyway."

"Well, that's a blessing, at least," Elinor laughed shortly. "But she's enough in herself to spoil the atmosphere. Surely you can see that, Meg?" She came to a halt in front of her sister. "And what about *you*? What sort of a life do you suppose you're going to have here, with Madam altering this and criticizing that? You won't have any authority in your own home any more. It's all much, much worse than we even imagined."

"I didn't expect to have any authority here, once Father's new wife was installed," Margaret said, as reasonably as she could. "It would hardly have been my right, you know."

"What *did* you expect, then?" retorted Elinor. "You were cheerful and optimistic enough about things yesterday. Were you just settling down cosily to the idea of being a cipher in your home, for goodness' sake?"

"No," said Margaret, with rather stiff lips. And she turned away, without trying to explain herself further. For Elinor's words had emphasized, with almost unbearable clarity, the brightness and freedom she had glimpsed yesterday, and the bleak and empty prospect to which everything had now been reduced.

Incredibly, dinner proved to be an uneventful and outwardly peaceful meal, in spite of all the electrical storms generated beforehand. It was true that Mr. Masters—handsome and rather overbearing at the head of the table—directed almost all his conversation to his wife. But John and the other unwelcome guest appeared to have patched up some sort of truce, for they contrived to cover cricket and the weather, travel and even some aspects of market gardening, with civility if not warmth.

"Men are extraordinary!" thought Margaret. "They can think the most unspeakable things of each other on business or professional grounds, and still do everything but slap each other on the back socially. All the same——" she glanced at her lovely elder sister, silent and glum at the other side of the table—"I wish Elinor would show just a fraction of that, instead of sitting there looking like the Tragic Muse on an off-day."

It was not until much later that evening that she managed to get hold of her brother alone. But then she ran into him in the hall and, catching him by the arm, she drew him into the now empty study and exclaimed:

"John, I must talk to you! What on earth has Father really arranged with Giles Ormby?"

"A full partnership, as far as I can make out," replied her brother, with admirable calm.

"But it's monstrous! What about you?"

"Me?" John looked genuinely surprised. "*I'm* not injured by anything Father is doing. I was rather incensed on behalf of you girls, at first. But later——"

"You're the most concerned, though," Margaret interrupted, full of zeal on his behalf. "After all, you're the only son, and even if your present interest happens to be——"

"Not my present interest, Meg," John interrupted in his turn, with good-humoured finality. "I know what you all think—even you, who are on the whole the most understanding of us all. You think I'm bound to come to my senses one day and decide that I prefer prosperous security in Father's firm to what he is pleased to call 'this crazy business with fruit and vegetables'. But that just isn't so, you know. I'm satisfied—more than satisfied—with what I'm doing. *This is what I want.* And, though I realize I'm unlikely ever to make more than a modest living out of it, I'm happy doing it. One can't be *more* than happy, Meg, even if one doubles or trebles one's income. Have you ever thought of that?"

She was silent for a moment, wondering if perhaps John had stumbled on a profound truth which escapes ninety-nine people out of a hundred. But then she felt bound to add:

"Dear, that's all right while you're on your own. But suppose you want to marry and have a family? A solid position means a great deal more to one then."

"Not if I marry a girl with my own outlook—and I don't think I could love anyone without it," he returned simply.

"Oh——" she laughed, half moved, half exasperated by the odd mixture of the wise and the unworldly which was so incredible in her father's son—"I haven't any other argument to oppose to yours. Only—it hurts me to feel that Father is closing the door against you."

"Don't be silly." John was unmoved. "You can't expect him to keep it open indefinitely. Why should he? At first I did flare up, because I thought he was pretty well casting off the whole of his own family, in favour of a stranger. But once Giles had come in and explained things more quietly——"

"Oh, he did that, did he?" She was glad that his unexpected intervention had been of real use.

John nodded. "He's not a bad chap, you know," he said reflectively. "Clear-sighted and reasonable. I could get along all right with him. But as for her——" John broke off and rubbed his chin meditatively.

But Margaret was not specially anxious to pursue the subject of Giles's reasonableness. Instead, she asked quickly:

"And what was it that he explained so—clearly and reasonably?"

"Well, it's true that Father is taking him into partnership, Meg, but on a perfectly sound and businesslike basis. Giles is putting substantial capital into the firm, at a time when it's definitely needed, it seems. In other words, Father would have had to find some sort of business partner within the next six or eight months, anyway. And the obvious choice is his stepson. I don't know that any of us can carp much at that. If Father hadn't married Giles's mother—whom none of us likes—I suppose we'd have taken him in our stride, as a business necessity."

"Yes, but——" Margaret frowned in an effort to remember just why the arrangement had seemed so undesirable, even menacing, only a matter of hours ago. "It's a very special position, John. A rather dangerous mixing of the personal and professional elements. We don't know anything about him—about either of them. Except that Father is obviously under her thumb at the moment. And she is the kind to shoulder one gently out of the way until she's in possession of everything she wants."

"We were talking of him," her brother reminded her

with a smile. "Would you have said that *he* was specially acquisitive—or unscrupulous?"

"N—no," Margaret admitted reluctantly. "But then we've known him only a matter of hours. How can we tell? And how shall we be able to tell in the future, come to that? It isn't as though any of us will know a thing about what is happening either in the foundry or in the office. If you were there——"

"No good, Meg!" John laughed and put up his hands, as though in self-defence. "Nothing will induce me to change my mind."

"I wasn't trying to change your mind. I was just thinking how—how undefended our whole position is, if he *should* prove to be a charming but unscrupulous go-getter." She broke off and sighed. And for a moment her brother watched her, with thoughtful and slightly narrowed eyes.

Then he said, more than half seriously:

"Weren't you saying, only yesterday, that you'd have to get a job and that you might go into the business? I advised against it then, on general grounds. But now—I don't know so much——"

He left the sentence unfinished. And, after a pause, she said, slowly and half to herself:

"That might be the answer, of course. It would mean that *one* of us was there—even if in a modest capacity. It would also be showing some degree of interest in Father's life-work. It could be a means of helping the whole situation and——"

"Would you simply hate it?" John asked curiously.

"Hate it? Oh, no." With difficulty, she resisted the impulse to say that she hardly cared what she did, now that Paul was no longer part of her life. But, biting back that negative and somewhat spineless statement, she went on with considerable resolution, "I think I might even grow to like it, John. I'd have to start at the very bottom, of course, and learn pretty well everything. But it could be an absorbing interest. It would help——"

"What would it help?" inquired her brother, as she paused and bit her lip.

She could not tell him that she hoped it might help to dull the ever-present ache at her heart. Instead, she declared firmly:

"It might help to make me feel useful again, instead of just the spare wheel in a strange household."

"Think it over——" John began.

But she shook her head, with sudden determination.

"No. I don't even need to think it over. It's the answer to—all sorts of things. And I think it will please Father. I'm going to ask him—now."

And, before her brother could offer any further advice about acting in less of a hurry, Margaret gave him a reassuring pat on the arm, and went in search of her father.

She found him alone in the drawing-room—Eileen having apparently already gone upstairs to bed—and it struck Margaret, as she came in, that although her father held a newspaper in his hand, he looked a little aimless and curiously isolated.

"Father——" she came over with a smile, "can I come and talk to you?"

"So long as you don't want to give me a list of reasons why you should take yourself off out of this house," he replied rather shortly, but he put aside his paper and seemed pleased to see her.

"Nothing like that," Margaret assured him, making a mental note of the fact that Elinor had evidently been saying her piece first. "I've been wondering——" she drew up a low stool and sat down near him—"What would you think of my having a job in the firm?"

"What sort of a job?" He sounded rather less than promising.

"The most modest there is, I suppose," she conceded with a laugh. "I realize I'd have to be a learner for some time. I suppose I could start by typing invoices—at least I can type—or something like that."

"When did you get this idea?" inquired her father,

though she saw that his reaction was not unfavourable.

"As soon as I heard someone else was going to be the mistress in this house," Margaret replied promptly. "Father, it just wouldn't be fair to Eileen to have me always here, you know. It's *her* household now. And nothing is more difficult for any woman than to have her predecessor around all the time. It cramps her style, and sometimes diminishes her authority."

Margaret did not really imagine Eileen allowing her style to be cramped or her authority diminished. But she had the sense to realize that her father, in his present mood, would much rather regard the problem from Eileen's point of view than her own.

Indeed, Mr. Masters looked at his second daughter with something as near relief as he was likely to permit on his face.

"Well, that's true," he agreed. "I must say you're the first to have talked much sense about the new arrangement."

"It *was* a bit sudden," Margaret murmured submissively. "You must give us time to get used to things."

"Elinor hasn't given herself much time," was the short reply. "She wants to take herself off to Newcastle and live on her own."

"It might be the answer, for the time being." Margaret stifled the thought of how much she would miss her elder sister. "Eileen might find it easier to get used to us in individual doses, rather than struggling to cope with a whole new family."

"You may be right." Obviously Mr. Masters saw his new wife as a gallant little woman endeavouring to keep her own end up against a hostile and firmly entrenched family.

"With Elinor reasonably happily established in Newcastle, Penelope at school, and John busy from dawn to dusk, she could have a very free run, provided I was out of the way."

"I told Eileen you would see things reasonably,"

declared Mr. Masters, thereby disclosing the fact that the gallant little woman had already spoken up smartly on her own behalf, and had herself given some suggestions for dealing with her all too numerous stepchildren.

"Well, then——" Margaret spoke determinedly without rancour—"it's obvious that I should get a job. I'm not specially qualified and would find it difficult to get one in the open market, I daresay. Whereas, in your office——"

"My business isn't a dumping ground for untrained workers," her father growled.

"I know. But practical experience on the spot would be much better than any academic training in a business school."

"Good heavens, yes!" Mr. Masters was a great one for practical experience. "So long as you don't get any inflated ideas, just because you happen to be the daughter of the boss, and are willing to start at the bottom——"

"I'm willing to start at the bottom," Margaret informed him quietly. "Though I don't propose to *stay* there. I shouldn't be your daughter if I did."

He laughed at that and pinched her cheek hard, but in a by no means displeased way.

"Well," he said genially, "when do you want to start?"

"On Monday," replied Margaret, without hesitation.

"Um-hm?" He raised his strongly marked eyebrows. "Neck and neck with Giles, eh?" And he gave her such a shrewd look that she knew perfectly well he was not insensible to the implications inherent in her sudden decision.

"Hardly that," she pointed out mildly. "He's starting at the top. I'm starting at the bottom. Our paths are not very likely to cross."

"Don't be too sure of that," her father replied dryly. "There are few watertight compartments in a business like mine. Which means, Meg, that you'd better make up your mind to get on with Giles."

"I shall get on with him," Margaret promised quietly, as she got to her feet. "And I'm glad you're willing to give me a trial, Father. We'll talk over the details during the weekend. It will give us a couple of days to get everything worked out."

A couple of days, however, proved too short a time to do more than lay down the lines for the many alterations which seemed likely to take place in the Masters household.

For one thing, Eileen was not specially pleased about her second stepdaughter's decision and said she had supposed Margaret would have been ready to help her out more at home.

Refraining from saying, "Not in a subordinate position, thank you," Margaret explained politely that she felt Eileen could make her many plans and alterations better on her own. And to this decision she pleasantly but firmly adhered. Giles, for his part, made no comment on Margaret's decision, though he did raise one eyebrow— to the intense admiration of Penelope.

It was Elinor who unexpectedly completed all *her* arrangements with a speed and exactness which suggested that her Newcastle plan had not been just the angry impulse of the moment. Indeed, it occurred to Margaret that perhaps she herself had not been the only one to cherish a secret dream and see the possibility of its fulfilment in the general upheaval.

Elinor cheerfully informed them that she had telephoned lengthily with a friend of hers in town, and that she had already decided to share a flat which the other girl was finding too large and expensive on her own.

"Can I come and stay with you sometimes?" demanded Penelope, who was pleasurably excited by all these changes because, in her own words, she liked "to have things happening".

"Of course." No one could be sweeter than Elinor when she was getting her own way. "Any of the three of you will be welcome at any time. You should find it specially useful to have a place to come to in town, Meg! Now that you won't be tied by household concerns, we can have some really gay evenings. I must look up various friends and acquaintances. That nice fellow who admired you so much, for one. Paul Freemantle. I'm sure——"

"No!" Margaret spoke more sharply than she had intended, nervously aware that Giles was in the room and could hardly fail to hear what they were saying.

"Oh, Meg, didn't you like him? I thought he was exceptionally charming. In fact, if he hadn't shown such a marked preference for you, I'd have given him some serious attention myself," Elinor declared lightly.

"Well, that's water under the bridge now." With a supreme effort, Margaret managed to say that casually and to dismiss the subject of Paul as of no more than passing importance. "I believe he's engaged to Hester Graham. You know—the Grahams who live in that lovely Georgian house near Bywell."

"You don't say?" Elinor looked interested. "Well, we'll gather plenty of other interesting company round us, once I'm established in my own place in town. I'll see you have fun when you come, Meg."

Margaret said that would be nice, and secretly felt grateful to Giles for not only continuing to read his paper, but also managing somehow to look as though he had not heard a word.

The weekend brought no further family clashes. On the other hand, nor did it do much for warmer or closer relations. Everyone was very polite to each other, but more in the manner of strangers at a hotel than people relaxing in their own home. And although Monday morning meant fresh stresses, and at least one separation, Margaret was almost relieved when it came.

"I'll come home tomorrow evening, Meg, to fetch some of my things," Elinor explained, "and probably one or two evenings after that. But tonight I'm going to stay with Dulcie and talk everything over. There's a lot to arrange."

"I'm sure," agreed Margaret, trying not to mind too much the sudden realization that the first break in the family structure was taking place. "But, Elinor, you—you will come home quite often, won't you? I mean——" There was a lump in her throat and she stopped.

"Why, of course!" Elinor hugged her with something between affection and impatience. "You're not going to lose me as easily as that. I was telling John as much, earlier this morning. It's just that, so long as we jogged along in the pleasant old family way, I never had more than a vague desire for independence. Now that a major change has been forced on us, I'm determined to turn it to my own advantage. Just like your starting in a job, you know," she urged her sister anxiously. "After all, that was *your* chance to break out of the domestic web, wasn't it?"

Margaret said she supposed it was. And then, as time was pressing, they exchanged a quick, and rather unusual, kiss and went their separate ways.

Mr. Masters was already in the driving seat of his car when Margaret came out of the house five minutes later. Giles was seated beside him and Penelope bouncing about on the back seat, lamenting loudly that only she was having no welcome change in the usual routine.

"Elinor in a flat of her own, and Margaret starting a business career!" she mourned. "And all I'm doing is going to stupid old school, as usual."

Fortunately, however, Dorothy Emms appeared just then, and Penelope gave a loud shriek of welcome and said couldn't they give Dorothy a lift too?

Good-humouredly, Mr. Masters opened the car door and called to Dorothy, who was giving an excellent imitation of not even knowing that a car was there. She immediately hopped in, however, taking care to explain that her mother had said she was not to ask for a lift.

"Oh, Dorothy, wiggle your ears," begged Penelope. "I told Giles you could do it. He's our new stepbrother," she added, throwing in that detail in parenthesis. "He can raise one eyebrow without the other, but he can't wiggle his ears. Do wiggle your ears, Dorothy."

But Dorothy said, in a rather prima donna-ish sort of way, that she couldn't do it with her hat on, which precipitated a lively argument that lasted the three or four minutes required to reach the school. Here the two little girls were decanted, and the car drove on, Margaret feeling increasingly nervous, however much she might assure herself that there was no need to do so.

The workshops and the furnaces lay some way back from the entrance gates, but Mr. Masters stopped the car first at the small office block which would, presumably, be the scene of Margaret's entry into business life.

Here Mr. Masters was greeted with respectful enthusiasm, and genuinely concerned inquiries after his health, by his immensely efficient, middle-aged secretary, Miss Brant. Giles was presented to her, and received with polite reserve, and finally Margaret—who already knew her well, of course—was handed over to her care.

"Start her at the very beginning, Miss Brant, just like any other junior," Mr. Masters instructed firmly. Then he and Giles went off to inspect the works, while Miss Grant said, with what appeared to be sincere pleasure :

"I'm very glad to have you in the office, Miss Masters. It will be gratifying for your father to have one of the family here."

"Only if I make good." Margaret smiled at her frankly. "But I'm prepared to work hard, Miss Brant—and I hope you'll have the time and patience to train me well."

"I'll train you all right." Miss Brant smiled too, but with a touch of grimness. "No one round here gets away with a half-done job, Miss Masters, I can tell you."

And, in less than half an hour, Margaret was made fully aware of the truth of this.

Of the five girls who worked under Miss Brant, not one was allowed to waste her time or present a slovenly job. It was not that she ever raised her voice much, or resorted to bullying tactics. It was that she belonged to that fast-vanishing race (from which so many of the best teachers were drawn) who could make one feel, by one word or look, that laziness or carelessness were about as attractive as dirt behind the ears.

It is possible that, among the girls who passed through her hands, there were some whose egos suffered a certain amount of suppression. But what they lost on the Freudian swings they gained on the day-to-day roundabouts, and unquestionably they were pleasanter in the home and more useful in the office in consequence.

This, then, was the instructress into whose hands Margaret's business career was consigned. And, although she did not know this yet, she was remarkably fortunate to have it so.

CHAPTER III

During the next few weeks, life in the Masters household settled down into its new routine, though not without a certain amount of friction and one or two near-crises. One of these almost involved the departure of Gloria in what she called "a high dungeon". But Margaret acted firmly as peace-maker, and the moment of danger passed.

With her authority unchallenged, and with a free hand in the matter of alterations, the new Mrs. Masters showed the pleasantest side of her nature. In other words, like most people, she could be charming when she was getting her own way.

On the other hand, neither Margaret nor her brother (nor even Penelope, when she noticed) could watch quite so much of the old life being swept away without some degree of resentment and regret. And, however much one may know that silence is golden—particularly when protests achieve nothing—it is not in human nature to refrain from sharp comment all the time.

Margaret was glad each day of her decision to find herself a job. Not only because she found the work truly absorbing, but because she realized that she simply could not have kept the peace with her stepmother if she had been exposed to the continual pin-pricks and implied criticism which life at home would have meant.

As it was, she left the house quite early each morning, with her father and Giles, and spent the rest of the day under the capable and down-to-earth direction of Miss Brant. Anything less like the approach of Eileen—the calculated sweetness which so often concealed a barb—it would have been difficult to find. Miss Brant dispensed few smiles and fewer compliments, but one always knew exactly where one was with her.

From the wisps of gossip and comment which drifted

her way, Margaret gathered that the other newcomer was also settling down well. Giles seemed popular with the men, on continued good terms with her father, and highly approved by any of the shorthand-typists he had occasion to employ.

Margaret ventured to comment on this once to Miss Brant. But that lady merely replied dryly, "Yes, he's working himself in well." Which left Margaret wondering if this were austere commendation, or a sardonic suggestion that he was in some way feathering his own nest.

One thing at least seemed certain. He was determined not to thrust himself upon the home circle. For, in spite of his mother's protests, he firmly set about finding a place of his own. And one Saturday afternoon—to Margaret's intense surprise and rather to her gratification—he asked her if she would drive out with him and see a property he had been offered.

"Willingly," said Margaret, who like most of her sex loved looking over houses. "But don't you think perhaps your mother is a—a better person to consult?"

"No," replied Giles, without amplification.

And, since that seemed to leave very little basis for discussion, Margaret fetched a coat and they drove out together through the cool April afternoon.

When they arrived, she immediately took to the sturdy, uncompromising little place, which had started as no more than a simple "two-up and two-down" stone cottage about sixty years before. But the last owner had added a bathroom upstairs and extra room downstairs, and the garden was exceptionally attractive.

She listened with amused attention while Giles walked round, opening doors and explaining how he intended to throw the two downstairs rooms into one big one, and convert the kitchen—with its brick floor and large open fireplace—into a sort of kitchen/dining-room.

"I think it could be lovely," Margaret agreed. "But, Giles, I hope you're not doing this because we—I mean——" She stumbled a little over the words, and then came out with the admission quite frankly. "I shouldn't like to think we'd driven you out of what is quite justly your home now, as well as ours."

"You haven't," he assured her crisply. "Any more than we have driven out Elinor. Let's be adult about this. I'm frankly glad of the excuse to have a place of my own. And so is Elinor, if you ask me."

"Well—yes," conceded Margaret reluctantly. For she had already been to see Elinor, who was revelling in the freedom of her new life, and she knew it would be disingenuous to pretend that the change meant any real hardship to her elder sister.

"I've wanted to have a place like this for years," he went on, with such feeling that Margaret exclaimed, before she could stop herself:

"Then why didn't you? At least—well, it's not my business, of course. But I'm rather surprised you didn't—break away before this."

"It wouldn't have been easy," he said curtly.

"No. I suppose it never is if——" She was going to say, "If one's mother is possessive." But wiser counsels prevailed and she made it, "If one is the only one."

Just for a second he hesitated. Then he said:

"I'm not the only one, Margaret. I have a sister, Maxine, who is about half a dozen years older than I am."

"Have you?" Surprised, Margaret did some rapid mental arithmetic, and came out with the discovery that Eileen must be rather older than she had supposed. "Then why doesn't anyone ever mention her? Does Father even know about her?"

"Probably not." Giles spoke quite coolly. "She married—much against my mother's wishes, and very shortly after my father died. Rightly or wrongly, Mother considered herself in some sense deserted by Maxine. That's why she came to depend on me a great deal, so that I could hardly—break away, as you put it, without hurting her afresh."

Margaret held her breath and counted ten. Then she

asked mildly, "Is your sister happily married?"

"Very." He smiled suddenly, as though some recollection pleased him. "I'm extremely fond of her, and I like her husband, Bernard—and they have two charming kids. I manage to see something of them from time to time."

"But your mother has nothing to do with them?"

"Nothing," he said, and the smile faded, and there was that slightly wary, shut-in look about him again.

"How horrible of her," exclaimed Margaret frankly.

"I think it's wrong—and very silly," Giles said unemotionally. "But you can't change people. Anyway, one of the reasons why I was interested in a business up here was that Maxine and her family live not so very far away. When I heard through a business contact that your father was looking for a partner, I got in touch with him and——"

"Oh, *that* was how you all met!" interrupted Margaret. "Somehow, I thought it was the other way round."

"How do you mean—the other way round?"

"Well, I thought your mother managed to meet—I mean met Father, and then you were the—the secondary consideration, as it were."

He grinned suddenly, as though he found that an amusing description of himself.

"No. I was the primary consideration—at first," he assured her. "Then, in the course of business discussion, I took your father home to meet Mother and—the rest followed."

"I—see." Margaret could not possibly have said why, but it seemed much less questionable that her father should have married the mother of his junior partner than that he should have gone into partnership with his new wife's son. It was just a question of a different emphasis, she assured herself. But an important one which made Giles's position much less suspect.

"What do you see, I wonder?" He looked amused and curious

But she could not possibly have explained either her suspicions or the lessening of them. So, instead, she said :

"Oh—nothing. Tell me, where does your sister live?"

"Near Morpeth, on the other side of Newcastle."

"I know it quite well! It's a charming market town," declared Margaret. "And what does her husband do?"

"He has a smallholding. Really, a very modest sort of place——"

Which explain's Eileen's objection to the marriage, of course! thought Margaret contemptuously, but she held her peace.

"——But they're very happy," Giles went on. "That's one thing that made me able to understand your brother's insistence on his market-gardening scheme. It's the same sort of idea. I sometimes think that people who work with the soil and with growing things tend to have a contentment and a sane sense of values that get lost somehow in other ways of life," he added reflectively. "It wouldn't suit me personally, but I do see that it has something basic about it that appeals irresistibly to some people. And they're nearly always nice people, what's more," he concluded.

"I suppose you're right." Margaret smiled, touched and pleased that anyone she regarded as worldly should speak so approvingly of John. "Tell me, does your mother know that Maxine and her family are comparatively near here?"

He shook his head.

"They've had no communication for a long time. Bernard was somewhere in the south when he and Maxine married. And Mother hasn't followed the course of their fortunes since."

Extraordinary and ridiculous woman! thought Margaret. But again she held her peace. For it was obvious that Giles was not prepared either to speak against his mother or to hear anyone else do so, and she supposed she could hardly blame him for that.

"But," Giles went on, "I'm not without some hope of

bringing them together. I don't mean that I've any sentimental expectation of their falling on each other's necks.
But sometimes I think Mother has her regrets——"

"Do you?" Margaret looked sceptical, for she thought
her stepmother was not one to *allow* herself any regrets.

"Oh, yes." Giles seemed unmoved by the tone of her
voice. "If one takes up an attitude—and Mother is apt to
—it's extremely difficult sometimes to find the way back
out of one's own foolishness."

"Rather the same as with children," Margaret said,
half to herself. "One should always give them the chance
of a way back, when they've been naughty."

"Exactly." He nodded—seemingly pleased with the
implication that there was something of the child in
Eileen. But, as that had not been at all what Margaret
meant, and she found it difficult to see her stepmother in
this indulgent light, she wisely reverted to the subject of
Maxine and remarked, quite sincerely :

"I should like to meet your sister. I think she sounds
nice."

"She is—and you shall." There was no doubt about his
pleasure this time. "I'll drive you over one weekend. I'm
sure——" he smiled suddenly—"that Maxine will be
both amused and charmed to meet a stepsister."

"O—oh, how—odd! I hadn't thought of it quite like
that," Margaret exclaimed. "But it's true, of course,"
she added. "How incredibly life has changed in the last
few weeks!"

"But not entirely for the worse? You do like working
at the foundry, don't you?" He sounded a little as though
he wanted her to discover some advantages to the new
arrangement.

"Yes. I can't pretend anything else," Margaret admitted frankly. "I like working under Miss Brant. She's
stimulating and marvellously good at training one.
Besides, I find the work unexpectedly absorbing, and
that's a—a help, in all sorts of ways."

"I understand," he said, and she supposed he did—

even more than she would have wished. For, as she had to remind herself again, the odd thing was that Giles—whose very existence had been unknown to her four weeks ago—knew more of her inmost thoughts and feelings than her own family did.

There were times when she resented this—when she would have given almost anything *not* to have him know about Paul's desertion and her own unhappiness. But there were other times when there was some sort of curious relief in the knowledge that she was not entirely isolated in her grief and dismay. That someone—even Giles Ormby—knew and was sorry and indignant on her behalf.

"So you like the place and think I should buy it?"

His question brought her back to the immediate present, as he held the door for her and they went out again into the open air.

"I think it's charming, and you won't do better," she assured him. "But I don't feel my opinion can be vital. Aren't you going to ask your mother to inspect it?"

"Not until I've bought it and converted it," he replied, with a quick, almost mischievous smile which showed the touch of the good-humoured rebel in him. "But I wanted a woman's views on the place before I bought it. I'm grateful for your opinion."

She told herself that he would have said as much to any girl he had brought to see the place. But something in the way he made the remark served to console her quite astonishingly for the disparaging attitude displayed by Eileen over so much of her housekeeping and management.

They drove the short distance home in companionable silence, to find that Mr. Masters and Eileen had gone out for the evening to friends.

"The master and her have gone out," was Gloria's somewhat unceremonious way of putting it. "And Mr. John's phoned to say he'll be late. And Penelope's in next door with young Dorothy, and Mrs. Emms says can she stay to supper?"

Then, before Margaret could decide if she were pleased or put out by the thought of dining alone with Giles, Gloria casually delivered the totally unexpected blow.

"There's a visitor for you," she remarked over her shoulder, as she made for the kitchen. "Mr. Freemantle came about ten minutes ago. I put him in the drawing-room and said you'd not be long. I guessed you wouldn't want to miss him like." For Gloria—far more than the family, of course—had been aware of Paul's frequent visits in happier days.

"Mr.—Freemantle?" gasped Margaret. "Are you sure?"

"Well, of course I'm sure. He was here often enough once," replied the outspoken Gloria. "Hung up his hat here, more or less, you could say." And she took herself off, leaving Margaret in such a state of indecision and dismay that she had absolutely forgotten Giles's presence until he said quietly:

"Do you want to see him?—or shall I get rid of him?"

"What?" She turned to him, startled and looking as though she hardly really saw him. "Oh—no. No, it's all right. I'll see him, of course. Only——"

"Only what?" he asked, as she paused helplessly.

"I don't want a—a long scene of explanations and—regrets. I simply couldn't bear that! If only I could get it over quickly—without his—his being remorseful and—sorry for me—and knowing how I feel——" She broke off and bit her lip. "Oh, why did he come? It would have been so much better——"

She stopped again, torn between the longing just to see him and the dread of humiliation and distress. Then, as she stood there, the picture of unhappy indecision, Giles touched her arm lightly and said, in a deliberately matter-of-fact tone:

"Go in and see him. Make it as brief and casual as possible. And if you like I'll barge in, all unawares, in about ten minutes' time. That will avoid any prolonged scene."

"Oh, *would* you?" She had forgotten that he was someone to be kept at a distance. He seemed simply the blessed means of avoiding too painful a scene with Paul. "If I knew there would be a time limit to it——"

"There will be. The scene will be quite short," he told her reassuringly. "Remember that, and keep a brave face on things."

He actually gave her a slight push towards the drawing-room. And, with an agitated whisper of, "Don't make it more than ten minutes," she went reluctantly towards the room where she had so often run eagerly to greet Paul.

When she opened the door and went in, he was sitting by the window. But he got up immediately, looking so exactly as he had always looked in those other stormy but wonderful days that her heart missed a beat, and she thought she could not go on.

"Meg——" He stood where he was, without even holding out his hand, and she saw that, for once in his life, the impulsive, confident, self-possessed Paul Freemantle hardly knew what to do.

Perhaps it was that which strengthened her. Or perhaps it was Giles's encouraging words, and the inner knowledge that, however painful this interview might be, he would terminate it in ten minutes' time. Anyway, she suddenly found the strength and resolution to come forward and say, quite composedly :

"Hello, Paul. I didn't expect to see you here again."

"No. I suppose I could have taken the more tactful—or cowardly—method of just letting you hear about things from someone else," he replied, faintly reassured by her calm, she saw.

"But I have heard. If you mean your engagement to Hester Graham." Even that she got out quite calmly. ·

"You *have* heard?" He seemed both relieved and dismayed. "But—how? The actual announcement was made only today."

"Was it? But news like that travels fast," she informed him carelessly.

"But I told no one from here. Hester and I particularly ——"

"Well, it doesn't matter, Paul, how I heard." She spoke almost gently. "Was that all you came to tell me? That you are now engaged to Hester Graham?"

"That was—the main thing." He thrust his hands into his pockets and stared at the floor. And, because she had never before seen him shamed and boyishly dismayed, she suddenly found him so heartbreakingly appealing in this mood that she wanted to cry:

Don't leave me! don't leave me! Now that I see you again I can't bear to let you go. I love you—You said you loved me. It can't be over! it can't—it can't——

But none of that could be said. She could only stand there, wordless and helpless, until he spoke again, in a slightly husky voice.

"Meg, I don't know how to explain—how to apologize——"

"You don't have to." As long as she could speak coldly and without emotion she could get the words out steadily. It was when his shamed look and his unfamiliarly uncertain tone tore at her heart that she found herself longing to break into pleading and despair. "These things—happen, don't they? They don't happen only to you, Paul."

She meant that generally, but he caught at it eagerly, and looked up with a light of hope in his face.

"You—know that? You mean you've discovered that too? Realized that perhaps we were not—not meant for each other?"

"That wasn't what I said."

"Oh——" the light died out of his face again, leaving it unhappy and oddly young-looking.

She told herself that it was not that she was sorry for him, it was just that she could not help loving him. She had no wish to reassure him, as such, for the lesson, however sharp, was deserved. Only, if he continued to look like that, she could think only how much she loved him, instead of realizing that this was a Paul to whom she was saying goodbye. So she made one more effort, and her voice was cool and self-controlled as she said:

"I appreciate your coming, Paul. But it wasn't necessary. I knew about the engagement already, and I had accepted the fact that you—that we were not really meant for each other, as you say. When we last saw each other——"

But no, she must not talk about those lost and lovely times. If she did she would begin to weep. And, as she thought that, she realized how perilously near tears were.

"When we tentatively discussed the future——" to such dry, ridiculous terms must she now reduce those passionate pleas and arguments—"we weren't very realistic, were we? Being apart so long has taught us both quite a lot." Only by slipping in that "both" could she preserve her pride and self-respect. She meant to include it without emphasis, but he seized upon it instantly.

"So you *did* find that too?" he insisted eagerly. "Meg——" he actually caught hold of her arm, in the intensity of his feeling, and she was horrified to discover the burning emotion which the mere touch of his fingers could engender in her.

"Please——" she gasped. "Leave me alone. Don't—don't touch me."

"But you must tell me!" Far from releasing her, he even drew her slightly towards him. "It's nothing to be ashamed of. Don't you see? I'm thankful to know there is someone else with you too. It makes me feel less of a heel. Who is it, Meg? Please tell me. Then I don't have to think of you as heartbroken and——"

"You don't have to think of me at all," she managed to say—angrily, despairingly.

"But I do! You're horribly on my conscience." He seemed to have no idea of how much *that* could hurt. "I'd be so glad to know what lucky fellow has succeeded me. Who is it, Meg?"

The worst nightmare could be no more appalling than this, she thought. With him so near, so insistent, she knew that at any moment she would forget everything else and just cling abjectly to him, weeping and begging him not to go. She must not—she *must* not——

And then, just as dear, familiar sounds can wake one from a nightmare, so the sound of the opening door told her that rescue was at hand, and, in that moment of unspeakable relief, she gasped the one word, "Giles!"

"Giles?" she heard Paul repeat in astonishment. And before she could say, "No, no! I didn't mean it that way!" he had turned to look at the newcomer.

"Giles Ormby!" he exclaimed, on a note of delighted recognition. "My dear fellow, I had no idea—I didn't know you and Margaret even knew each other. Much less that you——"

"His mother married Father—a few weeks ago," Margaret found herself babbling wildly, in a desperate attempt to interrupt him before he could say anything more damaging.

"But that's wonderful!" Paul, who had always prided himself on the quickness of his deductions, evidently felt he had sized up the situation completely. "Of course," he said, as he wrung Giles's somewhat reluctant hand, "it was *you* I told about Hester and myself. In the fullness of my heart, on the very day after we'd discovered that we loved each other. Then, later, we decided not to make any announcement until I could get north and tell Margaret first. How could I know that you, of all people, would be coming straight here? But that it should turn out this way! It's wonderful."

"Aren't you a bit excessive in your self-congratulation?" Giles said dryly. "You're extraordinarily cheerful about ditching one girl and getting engaged to another, surely?"

"Oh——" Paul did look dashed for a moment. "Don't think I haven't had sleepless nights over this and felt the most utter cad. But that's really why I'm so profoundly relieved to hear about you and Margaret——"

"Wait a minute," interrupted Margaret desperately, aware that Giles's alert glance was now on her, and that one eyebrow had gone up, in the way Penelope much admired. "I must explain——"

"No, *I'll* explain!" Paul interrupted good-humouredly in his turn. "It's my discovery, after all. When I came here to tell Meg about my engagement I was both horrified and relieved to find that she not only knew all about it, but was taking it with absolute calm—as though I didn't mean a row of beans to her anyway. She let me flounder in well-deserved discomfort for a while——" he shot a brilliant smile at the still, pale girl by the window— "and then admitted I was not the only one who had changed."

"Good," said Giles coldly.

"Even then," went on Paul, "it took me some time to get the name of the lucky fellow out of her. It was only just as you came into the room that she said, 'It's Giles'."

"I didn't say that," Margaret exclaimed. "You don't understand——"

"He's got the general drift of things, Meg," said Giles, calmly and unexpectedly. "The details don't matter. And, as I said before you came in, this isn't a scene one need prolong."

"But Paul has misunderstood completely! I didn't mean——"

"*What?*" For one horrified instant, Paul seemed to glimpse the appalling possibility that he had made a mistake. "But you said—Lord, don't say I've humiliated you even further!"

He looked at her in momentary pity and dismay, so deep that it seemed to scorch her, so that she could have cried aloud in almost physical agony. Then Giles's voice interrupted, with heavenly coolness and self-possession :

"Don't start jumping to wild fresh conclusions, Freemantle. You got it right the first time."

"You mean——" Paul passed his handkerchief over

an obviously damp forehead—"that Margaret—that you and Margaret——"

"I mean that you're quite right in supposing you're not the only one to have had second thoughts," Giles said firmly. "It was a happy coincidence that you let me into your secret some weeks ago, for that made me able to assure Meg that she and I were free to take our happiness too."

"I see, I see." Paul was almost breathless with relief. "So that, of course, was how you came to tell her about Hester and me?"

"Of course," said Giles coolly. "Why else should I bother to tell her a piece of chit-chat about an acquaintance of mine who, as far as I knew, she didn't even know? Only when she said she was more or less engaged to you did I have the pleasure of telling her that, on the contrary, you were busily getting yourself engaged to someone else."

The irony of that did make Paul flush.

"All right. I'm not proud of myself," he muttered annoyedly. "Only relieved. Heavens, how relieved!"

He turned to Margaret as though suddenly finding Giles's rather sardonic little smile difficult to withstand.

"Meg dear, I hope you'll be wonderfully happy. Am I forgiven?"

"Of course." She wished she could have said that confidently, instead of whispering it. But she could only hope that he thought her overcome with emotion.

"And your heart's not broken?" he insisted teasingly. "Or at least, mended better than new by Ormby?"

"Oh, please——" Margaret pulled her hand away from his warm clasp. And, because there was no one else to whom to turn, she turned rather helplessly to Giles.

"All right, darling," said Giles with perfect composure. "He's only teasing you." And, putting his arm round her, he actually drew her against him. "And now that all the congratulations and apologies have been exchanged, I know you won't mind my telling you that Meg and I would rather like the rest of the evening to ourselves. We were planning an early dinner and a run into town."

"Of course." Nothing could have been more obvious than Paul's satisfaction that this interview was well over. "Goodbye, Meg. Let's exchange our good wishes—and kiss, to show there's no ill feeling."

She knew she could not possibly do that, and she shrank slightly against Giles at the very idea. He must have felt the small, involuntary movement, for he said, pleasantly but firmly:

"Sorry. You must allow me an old-fashioned streak of possessiveness. Meg's kisses are exclusively for me now. Aren't they, darling?" And he looked down at her and laughed.

Somehow, she managed to smile and nod her head. And then—with an attention to convincing detail which she found excessive—he bent his head and kissed her lightly, but with a smiling tenderness which must have convinced Paul at last that he really was the unwanted third.

She heard him repeat his laughing goodbyes. Then, as she remained very still in the circle of Giles's arm, she heard Paul's retreating footsteps as he went out of the room, and out of her life. And, after a moment, there was the sound of the front door closing.

He was gone—finally and irretrievably.

She was not sure if that was why she cried, or whether it was the dismayed realization of the fresh dilemma she had brought upon herself. Whatever the reason, the tears came pouring down. And, wrenching herself away from Giles, she dropped down in a chair and, covering her face with her hands, she wept. With anguish, disappointment, shame, or relief—she was not sure which.

For a minute or two he let her cry. Then he said, briskly though not unkindly:

"All right, it's over."

"I'm sorry," she whispered feverishly. "I'm sorry. It's partly the relief, I think, and partly—Oh, I don't know what on earth I'm to say to you!" She did raise her head

then, and found him regarding her with something between concern and, incredibly, a sort of amusement. "It's
not *funny!*" she gasped angrily.

"No, I know. And please don't think I'm not sorry for
your distress. But we're more or less engaged, you know,
at least in Freemantle's eyes—and I must say you're taking it very badly."

"Oh, we're not! And I never said we were. Truly, truly
I didn't. It's all so stupid. He got this—this idea that there
was another man and—and, in a way, I was almost glad
for him to think so, because it made my pride feel less
scorched. Then he tried to make me name the man and
he—he took hold of me, and I was desperate—and then
you came in and I just said your name, because I was so
unspeakably thankful that you'd come and——"

"Were you?" he interrupted softly. "I'm glad."

"Yes, but don't you see? He thought I was answering
his question when I said your name. He thought I was
naming *you.* And he was so relieved that he jumped to all
sorts of wild conclusions, perhaps a bit because he wanted
to. He *wanted* to be assured that he wasn't the only one
who—who fell out of love. Oh, it's too dreadful, and I'm
more sorry than I can say to have involved you like this.
You played up splendidly—almost too well—and now
look where it's landed you."

"But you don't have to keep on apologizing." He
laughed with what seemed to be genuine amusement, and
came and sat down on the arm of her chair. "Don't you
remember? I offered to help you in the very beginning,
when you first told me. I said perhaps I might save your
pride a bit by appearing to be a fresh admirer. And very
smartly did you brush me off, now I come to think of it,"
he added, with a meditative little smile.

"Oh, but I didn't take you seriously. You surely
couldn't have thought *that* was what I was thinking
about, when you came in and found Paul more or less
babbling about our engagement?" She was horrified at
the idea.

"I don't know what I thought," he admitted good-humouredly. "I just realized that I'd been cast as 'the other man', and I certainly wasn't going to let you down by refusing the role."

"But you couldn't have meant to be caught up in anything like this," she insisted. "It's terribly, terribly kind of you to have backed me up in an awkward situation, but you couldn't possibly have realized it would lead to—this,"

"Oh, come," he protested. "It's not as desperate as all that. We haven't actually got the banns up yet. If Freemantle thinks we're drifting towards an engagement—or even got it fixed—he has no special reason to broadcast the fact."

"He's bound to tell Hester," she countered quickly.

"That's true. But she doesn't live in Cromburgh."

"She doesn't have to! You come from London, so you have no idea what it's like in a district of this kind. News, views and gossips are exchanged at every tea-party. We live on a grapevine that's more efficient than any secret service. And, what's more, Paul probably knows at least a dozen people who move in Elinor's Newcastle circle. It will be all over the place in——"

"Listen, my dear——" he was very calm and masculine—"you're just getting panicky about nothing and ——"

"I'm *not* getting panicky," she retorted rather crossly. "I just don't know what to do next."

"Well, I'll tell you." He laughed and patted her shoulder reassuringly. "We'll do exactly what we told Paul we meant to do. We'll dine early—or rather, no! We'll dine in town, and have a pleasant relaxed evening after all this excitement. Go and wash your face, there's a good girl, and put on your prettiest dress. And I'll tell Gloria that we too shall not be in this evening."

"But Penelope! What about her?" Intrigued though she was by the thought of an unusual treat, Margaret could not forget her home responsibilities even now.

"Penelope's to have supper with the egregious Dorothy Emms, don't you remember?"

"Oh, yes, of course. And as long as Gloria sees she's back and in bed by nine-thirty—I'll have to let Mrs. Emms know she can stay." Margaret was already drying her tears and doing some running repairs to her face. "I'd better run in next door now. Do I look as though I've been crying?"

"You'd better not, or they'll think I've been beating you! Let me see.—No, you look rather nice, as a matter of fact," he told her unemotionally. "Come on, let's go and tell the Emms household that Penelope is theirs for the evening."

She laughed slightly and protestingly.

"You needn't come too."

"I like to come too," he assured her. "I have a secret passion for Dorothy, and hope she'll teach me how to wiggle my ears."

"You're absurd." She laughed again—with a touch of genuine amusement that time. "I think I can hear our two in the front garden. We'll go and see if Mrs. Emms is there too."

Mrs. Emms—spectacled like her daughter and at least as observant—was there, weeding industriously, while Penelope and Dorothy wrangled amiably over some dejected-looking tulips which they were steadily killing with kindness.

As Margaret and Giles appeared, however, they all downed tools—including Mrs. Emms—and straightened up as though pulled by strings. Then Penelope came bounding across to the low fence between the two gardens, crying in a voice shrill with excitement:

"Is it true? Is it true? Mrs. Emms wouldn't let me come in and ask because she said you wouldn't want to be disturbed. But is it true what that nice Mr. Freemantle said?"

"What," asked Margaret rather fearfully, "did that nice Mr. Freemantle say?"

"Why, that you and Giles are going to get married. He seemed terribly pleased about it—and so am I. I think it's a splendid idea, and can Dorothy and I *both* be bridesmaids, please? because we're *exactly* the same height."

There was an odd little silence. Then Giles said very softly beside Margaret, with a hint of laughter in his voice which she thought misplaced:

"Yes, I see what you mean."

CHAPTER IV

For a few moments Margaret stared, wordless, at the two eager, questioning little girls in front of her. She was also profoundly aware of Mrs. Emms—looking discreet, but obviously all ears—in the background. Then finally she managed to say :

"You—misunderstood Mr. Freemantle, Pen. He was just joking."

"Oh, he *wasn't*!" Penelope assured her eagerly. And Dorothy wagged her head knowledgeably and confirmed, "Oh, he wasn't joking. He was quite serious. Only very pleased. He said it was the best news he'd heard for a long time."

Evidently the theory of the joke was not going to work. But as Margaret's powers of invention failed, Giles came to the rescue, casually and pleasantly.

"Let's say he was exaggerating a little, Penelope—teasing you perhaps. Whatever Margaret and I have been discussing it certainly wasn't the question of bridesmaids."

"Nothing like that at all," insisted Margaret firmly, aware that half-measures were little good with Penelope. "Just forget about the whole thing."

"Oh, but we couldn't—could we, Dorothy?" Penelope appealed to her friend, who shook her head resolutely over the impossibility of forgetting anything so thrilling. "It was so exciting, you know," Penelope went on. "And then—it explained about your going together to look over houses."

"Going to look over houses?" repeated Margaret faintly.

"Yes. You *have* been looking over houses this afternoon, haven't you ? Mrs. Emms's cousin saw you going into one."

At this point, Mrs. Emms—whose talent lay rather in

the direction of relaying news than inventing it—came hastily forward.

"Margaret, I hope I haven't been indiscreet, and of course I wouldn't have said a *word* if Mr.—Mr. Freemantle, isn't it?—hadn't said what he did. It sort of—connected things in my mind, you know. And I remarked —really, just on the impulse of the moment—that that must have been why Felicity saw you going into Laureldean Cottage together. I know one shouldn't put two and two together so soon—"she beamed at them both—"and of course I know, much better than the children, that there's a time for saying things and a time for keeping one's own counsel—Now, girls——" she turned sharply to the two open-mouthed little girls—"you heard what Margaret said! Just forget about this, for the time being."

"For how long?" inquired her literal-minded offspring.

"Until I tell you to remember," replied Mrs. Emms promptly. "I'm so sorry, Margaret, if we were all tactless. But Mr. Freemantle did seem quite serious. I thought he *might* be teasing Penelope, of course, but——"

"He wasn't teasing me," stated Penelope, with the single-minded obstinacy of a mule. "He said, 'Hello, Penelope,' and I said, 'Hello, Mr. Freemantle, what are you doing here?' and he said, 'I came to tell your sister Margaret that I'm engaged, and, would you believe it? she had the same news for me.' So of course I said, 'What do you mean?' and he said, 'She's engaged too,' and I said, 'I know,' because I wasn't going to let him think he knew more about my own sister than I did. And then he said, 'Lucky Giles Ormby,' and I said——"

"Well, never mind what you said after that," interrupted Giles, rousing himself from the almost hypnotic state to which Penelope's style of reporting had reduced them all. "Just forget it all, as Mrs. Emms says."

"I don't want to forget about being a bridesmaid," said Penelope sulkily. "I've never been a bridesmaid and nor has Dorothy, have you?"

"No. But I'd like to be," agreed Dorothy, who was a great one for making her wishes clear. "And I don't mind waiting, and nor does Penelope, do you?"

Both were obviously prepared to go on interminably corroborating each other's statements, so Margaret broke in ruthlessly:

"*No one* is being a bridesmaid at the moment. But if ever the occasion arises, you both shall be. Now that's enough."

Then, while Penelope and Dorothy hopped up and down ecstatically, Margaret gratefully accepted Mrs. Emms's offer to keep Penelope for supper, and found herself blushing idiotically as she felt bound to add that she and Giles were going out, and that Gloria would expect Penelope in by nine-thirty.

"That's right, you two go and enjoy yourselves. You're only young once," declared Mrs. Emms, in the genial tone of one who believed in engagements, however secret, being celebrated. "And I'm sorry if we were a little —what shall I say?—*previous*. But we women are all the same, I suppose." She laughed deprecatingly. "We all love a wedding."

"Can we have wreaths of forget-me-nots and roses?" began Dorothy, at this fresh mention of the word "wedding". But Margaret turned and fled into the house, leaving Giles to deal with the question of the bridesmaids' headdresses.

"And to think——" she excaimed later, as they drove through the soft April evening—"to think that, of all people, Mrs. Emms's wretched cousin Felicity should be the one to see us go into Laureldean Cottage, and draw her ridiculous conclusions."

"Perhaps she didn't really draw any conclusions," Giles suggested magnanimously. "It was just a case of Mrs. Emms putting two and two together—her words, if you remember—after Paul Freemantle had opened his big mouth."

"You don't know Felicity Prendergast," was all Margaret replied, but in a tone that deterred Giles from seeking further enlightenment.

They drove in silence for a while, and then suddenly he began to laugh.

"It's not really funny," Margaret admonished him. "At least——" and then she also began to laugh, though more reluctantly. "What is so specially amusing?" she wanted to know.

"Mostly the thought of Dorothy Emms wreathed in forget-me-nots and roses, I think," he replied. "Though perhaps we should take the whole thing in a lighter mood than we've allowed ourselves up to now."

"I can't," Margaret said with a sigh. "I keep on thinking of having to explain finally—to lots of interested people—that the whole misunderstanding started with my trying to save my face when Paul Freemantle jilted me."

"I'm sorry," he exclaimed. "I keep on forgetting that this has a tragic side for you. But that particular admission at least you shall never make."

"I might have to. You never know how far explanations are going, once you start them."

"Then don't start them," he replied impatiently. "If it seems to you that the simplest thing is to go ahead with what we've begun—and extricate ourselves from it later—I'm willing to co-operate."

She turned in her seat to stare at him in astonishment.

"Exactly what do you mean by that?" she inquired.

"Just what I said. If we've somehow arrived at an engagement, or a half-engagement, or a possible engagement—or whatever it is—it might be simpler to accept the fact, and then, presently, like all people who find they have made a mistake, we can dissolve it without rancour on either side. *You* can jilt *me*, if you like——" he turned his head and grinned at her mischievously. "Or, if we do it by mutual consent, no one's pride is involved."

"Don't be ridiculous," was all Margaret had to say to this handsome offer. "I can't imagine that anything as elaborate as that would be required."

"No?" He looked reflective. "Well, perhaps you're right. Though you may remember that you also couldn't imagine that it would be necessary for me to pretend to be a new admirer of yours. But it was. And, if you want the truth, I'm playing the part with distinct enjoyment."

"Is this what you call 'taking the whole thing in a lighter mood'?" she inquired dryly.

"It could be."

And at that she laughed. But she refused to pursue the matter further and they talked then of other things.

By mutual agreement, they decided that the evening was too lovely to spend in town, after all. And so they drove to the coast and dined—rather luxuriously, she could not help thinking—at a window table in the best hotel at Witley Bay, overlooking the sea.

It was difficult for her to remember afterwards why the conversation went so smoothly, or the time so swiftly. They touched on so many topics, finding satisfying agreement on some and stimulating differences on others. And, by the time they finally rose to go, only the white edges of the waves could be discerned on the darkened sea; though the cheerful beam of light from St. Mary's lighthouse flashed out at regular intervals into the lonely night.

"Oh, it's been—lovely!" she exclaimed involuntarily, as they started for home. Though what she really meant was that it had been a wonderfully peaceful interlude, unexpectedly snatched from a rather troubled existence.

And she supposed—though she did not say so—that it was something of a tribute to Giles that he could make her forget so much, on the very day she had said her final goodbye to Paul.

As they neared Cromburgh again, however, she found herself wishing rebelliously that she were really going home—to home as she had known it for so many years. Now, inevitably, she felt it was Eileen's house, and she herself only there on polite sufferance.

But then she told herself impatiently not to be self-pitying. And, while Giles stayed to put away the car, she went on into the house, where she saw there was a light on in the drawing-room, showing that her father and Eileen must have returned from their evening engagement.

Deliberately schooling herself to be pleasant, she went in—to find her father slumped down in his chair and not looking specially pleased with life, while Eileen, still in her charming fur jacket, stood by the fire, with her arm along the mantelpiece.

She turned, as Margaret entered, and although her tone was deceptively mild, there was something indefinably hostile about her as she said :

"Why, Margaret, we wondered where you were. You're late, aren't you ?"

Margaret, who was not used to having her comings and goings questioned, slightly raised her eyebrows.

"Am I ? Giles and I drove to the coast and had dinner at the Rex. What did you and Father do ?"

"We dined with friends." There was a slight pause. Then Eileen said, with careful lack of emphasis, "We dined with the Grahams, at Fernwood Grange."

"The—Grahams ?—of Fernwood Grange," repeated Margaret rather stupidly, and suddenly she wished that Giles would come. "I didn't know we—we knew them."

"I met Mrs. Graham some while ago, in London," Eileen explained carefully. "I hadn't realized they were living so near until she telephoned this afternoon. Then, of course, we felt we should like to get together again as soon as possible. They're charming people. There's a daughter, Hester. She's just got engaged."

"So I heard." Somehow Margaret got that out quite calmly. "To Paul Freemantle, isn't it ?"

"Yes. He called in while we were there," said Eileen, with an air of significance there was no ignoring.

"Oh ?" said Margaret, because there was simply nothing else she could think of to say.

But Mr. Masters, who had been fidgeting annoyedly during this conversation and evidently finding it absurdly far off the mark, struck in at this point with characteristic directness.

"What's this about you and Giles?" he wanted to know.

And at that moment, to her overwhelming relief, Giles came into the room and inquired coolly, "What about us?"

"Father and Eileen have been dining with the Grahams," Margaret explained rapidly. "And—Paul Freemantle called in."

Her eyes were wide and anxious. But if Giles detected the signal of distress, he took it very calmly.

"Oh, yes?" He looked inquiringly at his mother. "And what had Paul Freemantle to say?"

"Giles!" Eileen allowed her hands to come together in a gesture faintly suggestive of her wringing them, and into her voice there crept a note of pathos which obviously distressed her husband. "Giles, I can't possibly suppose that what he said was *true*. You—you wouldn't let me hear news like that from a stranger, darling, would you?"

"I don't know, Mother." Giles spoke in his most matter-of-fact tone. "I haven't heard yet what news you heard from the stranger."

"Oh, Giles——" She would still have gone round and round the point if left to her own devices, Margaret saw. But Mr. Masters once more interrupted impatiently.

"Tell the boy outright, Eileen, and stop tormenting yourself. This Paul Freemantle—whoever he is, though I think I've seen him here with Meg once or twice—has got hold of some story that you and Margaret are secretly engaged."

Instinctively, Margaret moved towards Giles in this moment of finding that her worst fears were justified. And he, just as naturally, slipped his arm round her, as he said smilingly:

"Well, Meg, how much do we tell them?"

"Wh—whatever you think best," she stammered, with the frightening feeling that she was resigning the direction of her life into other hands, but that there was absolutely nothing else she could do at the moment.

"All right——" he turned to the other two, still smiling and self-possessed—"there's nothing secret about it. It's just that Freemantle jumped the gun a bit. Of course we should have told you ourselves, in our own good time ——"

"In your own good time!" interrupted his mother, on a note that would have been a reproachful wail if she had not been so obviously angry. "What do you mean by that? Oh, Giles, how *could* you let her do this to me? Keeping it all so secret—and then telling a complete stranger before your own mother! And—and even going and looking over houses before you gave a hint——"

And Eileen—who possessed the maddening gift of being able to cry most attractively—allowed two slow tears to trickle picturesquely down her cheeks.

"Now, my dear, don't distress yourself——" Mr. Masters was on his feet at once and ready to comfort her. "I suppose they were no more secretive about their plans than you and I were about ours. Now that we know——"

"*I* wasn't secretive!" retorted Eileen, with quivering lips. "I told my boy *everything*."

"The deuce you did?" Mr. Masters looked not altogether pleased by this piece of information. "Well, I didn't. I got the thing done and then I told my family ——"

"Which only shows where Margaret got her horrible secretive ways," burst out Eileen, forgetting to be pathetic and sounding astonishingly vicious. "Anyway, it's different for you. Giles is my only son——"

"Also, Mother," interrupted Giles, on a note no one had ever heard in his voice before, "Margaret is the girl to whom I'm engaged. I'll hear nothing against her— from you or anyone else."

"But I'm so *upset*——" Eileen was all pathos again. "You never kept anything from me before."

Giles neither challenged nor confirmed that, Margaret

noticed. Instead, still in his most matter-of-fact tone, he said:

"Look, Mother, one can't always time these things to suit everyone. Margaret and I had just—come to a decision, as you might say, when Paul Freemantle called in. He'd come to tell Margaret about his engagement—they're quite old friends, I understand. It was the most natural thing in the world that we should burst out with our news too."

"But what about your looking over houses?" Eileen asked accusingly, and Margaret had the impression that, if Giles had been given to swearing, he would have sworn at that moment.

"It wasn't 'houses', Mother. It was one inoffensive little cottage that I thought of buying."

"So you took *Margaret* to see it?" There was no disguising how that rankled.

"I took Margaret to see it," he agreed dryly. "Maybe that was what first gave us the certainty that we wanted a home together."

"You mean——" his mother still sounded accusing rather than congratulatory—"it all happened this afternoon?"

"It all happened this afternoon," he agreed gravely, "and that's why we couldn't tell you before. Cross my heart, that's the absolute truth. Isn't it, Meg?"

Margaret said it was, and tried to look like a girl who had been swept off her feet into a happy engagement.

There was a moment of heavy silence. Then Eileen said, with undisguised distaste:

"So you're really—engaged?"

"We really are," her son agreed. "Eh, Meg?" and he glanced at the girl in the circle of his arm and smiled.

It was absolutely impossible to say, "No, we're not, and this is all utter nonsense." Equally, it was impossible to explain away everything—even perhaps give the exact truth—if the whole story were inevitably to go back, via the Grahams, to Paul.

And so, with only the faintest moment of hesitation, Margaret found herself saying :

"Yes, we're engaged. And if the whole thing is rather surprising and sudden to you, I can only say that it's rather sudden and surprising to us as well, isn't it, Giles?"

Perhaps he hadn't quite expected that flash of concealed humour from her. At any rate, he gave a quick laugh of unfeigned delight and bent to kiss her.

"It's the most exciting and enchanting surprise that ever came my way," he declared, on a note of such sincerity that she was afraid he was enjoying himself much more than he should.

Mr. Masters, for his part—now reassured that his sensible daughter had been doing nothing silly behind his back—became suddenly genial and open-hearted.

"Well, Meg," he exclaimed, patting her on the shoulder and kissing her quite fondly, "I can't raise any objection to the family you want to marry into, can I?" And he laughed. "Come, my dear——" he turned to the still angry and woebegone Eileen—"You'd better give them both a kiss, and admit that you're very satisfied, now the whole thing has been explained."

For a second Eileen Masters looked at her husband as though she wondered, for the first time, why she had married him. Then Margaret saw her make a tremendous effort to recover her usual air of sweet understanding. She composed her features into a wistful smile and said :

"I still feel a *little* hurt, I must say. But I suppose it's not in young people to think of anything but their own happiness. I do hope you'll both be very happy." But Margaret at least noticed that the delicate emphasis on "hope" suggested that she feared the reverse.

"We shall be," declared Giles. And his coolly positive tone suggested that he already saw them, in his mind's eye, sharing a happy future together. A circumstance which caused some disquiet to Margaret as well as Eileen —though on slightly different grounds.

"Well, now that we've got everything explained, suppose we go to bed." Mr. Masters put his arm round his wife and would have drawn her away towards the door.

But Eileen stood her ground with astonishing determination, though her tone was plaintive as she exclaimed :

"Just a moment, darling, *please*! You can't hurry me away like that. I should like to stay and have a little talk with Giles—naturally."

"Not 'naturally' at all," her husband assured her, with misplaced amusement. "You haven't taken in the situation even now, my dear. It's *Margaret* who is entitled to the little talks with Giles now. Our business is to wish them goodnight and leave them to a cosy chat by the fire."

The unpalatable truth could not have been more plainly put, and Eileen, Margaret saw, had the greatest difficulty in digesting it with any semblance of good grace.

She kissed her son, with a lingering wistfulness more suited to a long farewell than affectionate congratulations. Then, with a glance of dislike which she simply could not conceal, she gently bumped her cheek against Margaret's, in her favourite simulation of a kiss.

"Goodnight, Margaret dear," she said. "Perhaps it isn't for me to say it, but you're a very lucky girl."

Margaret said gravely, and with some lack of truth, that she knew she was. Then, with the utmost reluctance, Eileen followed her husband out of the room.

Several seconds of silence succeeded their departure, and it was not until the sound of the two sets of footsteps died away on the stairs that Giles drew a long breath and said softly—as though they still might be overheard :

"It doesn't seem to be quite our evening, does it ?"

"Oh, *dear*!" Margaret ran both her hands through her hair, making it stand up round her head in a distracted but oddly becoming halo—"Why did she have to know Mrs. Graham, of all people ?"

Furious though she felt with Eileen's behaviour, this was the only form of criticism she felt she could permit herself to Eileen's son. But evidently her inward feelings imparted some acidity to the exclamation, for he replied, rather dryly:

"Why did you have to get involved with Paul Freemantle, of all gossiping idiots?"

"He *isn't* a gossiping idiot!" Tired and frightened as she now was, she knew that her retort was on the edge of provocative, but she could not help it. "We deliberately built up this story for him. What do you *expect* him to have done when he met my father and your mother? Keep it coyly to himself, for no reason whatever?"

"He might at least have used a little normal discretion."

"Oh, don't be stupid! You know perfectly well——"

"Darling, how right you are—and I adore you!" exclaimed Giles unexpectedly. And, before she could recover from her angry astonishment, he had caught her lightly round the waist and drawn her down on to the sofa beside him.

"What on earth——" she began, but he stopped her angry words with a kiss. And at that moment Eileen drifted gently into the room, murmuring:

"I'm sorry to interrupt, my dears. But I think—yes, there they are!—I left my gloves."

While she picked up her gloves, waved them gracefully in the direction of the sofa and discreetly took herself off again, Margaret remained, quivering with anger and fright, in the circle of Giles's arm.

Then he whispered—close to her ear and with much too obvious a note of laughter in his voice:

"You mustn't quarrel with me yet, Meg. That's not in the script. That comes much later—when we've decided to break things up. Just now you're supposed to think me pretty well right about everything. And, if you want to add a little good local colour to this scene, I think you might kiss me. After all, I've done it all up to now."

"I don't *want* to kiss you," Margaret whispered back fiercely.

."Not even though, as a kind of stepbrother, I've got you out of a nasty hole?" he retorted teasingly.

Perhaps it was the comforting reminder that he was, in some sense a stepbrother—surely a very safe relationship! —or perhaps it was the sudden realization that, but for him, she would have been overwhelmed by humiliation and despair by now. Whatever the reason, she experienced a sense of shame for her irritation and a glow of gratitude for his help. And, turning her head, she kissed his cheek and said rather humbly:

"Thank you, Giles."

"Oh, Meg——" his surprised, pleased laugh showed that he had not really expected any such reaction—"you really are a dear girl. I'm sorry you've been involved in all this, and perhaps someone else would have handled it better than I have. But I did the best I could—and I'll stand by you absolutely until this business is cleared up."

"No one else could have handled it better," she told him sincerely. "And I'm sorry I was cross and ungrateful. It's just that——"

"Forget it!" He gave her a quick, warm, but blessedly unsentimental kiss, which was extraordinarily comforting. "You've been through enough this evening to make most girls run up the wall."

"It was nice having dinner together, though," she murmured.

"Was it, dear?" He laughed and sounded pleased again. "Well, I'm glad that at least there was that decent interlude. If the reception scene when we got home has made you jumpy, I more than understand."

"I'm not cross any more," Margaret assured him. "I'm truly grateful. But——" with difficulty she smothered a sudden yawn—"I'm ghastly tired all at once."

"You have every right to be, after all the strain and excitement," he said. "It's time you were in bed."

"Do you think we've stayed down long enough to satisfy our respective parents' idea of an engaged couple's cosy chat?" inquired Margaret, and her faint smile showed that she was beginning to recover her usual calm and good nature.

"I should think so. I'm no more up in these things than you are, never having been engaged before," he told her, with a touch of humour. "Anyway, we can make our rules in this game, provided we keep up a façade of devotion in front of people."

"It's a formidable assignment. But—oh, dear, I'm sorry——" she smothered another yawn—"I just can't tackle anything else until tomorrow morning."

"Then don't try." He got up and, taking her hand, pulled her lightly to her feet. "We'll call it a day. And what a day! Go on upstairs, and I'll put out the lights."

"Leave the hall one. John isn't in yet," she said. And, at the mention of her brother, she realized with a stab of dismay that family explanations were by no means over.

But Giles is right. I'll think of all that tomorrow, she told herself. And, bidding her new fiancé an unemotional —indeed, almost absent-minded—goodnight, she went away upstairs to bed.

Alone at last in her own room, she felt vaguely that she ought at least to review her impossible position and see if, even now, there were not some escape from it. But, the moment she was in bed, utter weariness overcame her again. And, even as she tried to sort out the events of the afternoon and evening, she fell deeply asleep.

She carried with her into unconsciousness a confused impression of the anguish of Paul's departure, the comfort of Giles's support, and a singularly clear recollection of Eileen looking at her with something like hate in her eyes, and saying, "Perhaps it isn't for me to say it, but you're a very lucky girl."

Contrary to all probability, Margaret slept peacefully until morning. And, when she finally roused herself to brilliant sunshine, her first reaction was one of content and well-being rather than perplexity and dismay.

She lay there for a moment or two, drifting comfortably between sleeping and waking. Then suddenly, all that had happened swept back upon her, and it was no longer possible to lie there passively, waiting for further events to overtake her.

Hastily dressing, she went downstairs—to find a quiet house, with the hush of Sunday relaxation upon it. No one seemed to be about. But the french windows of the drawing-room stood open and, beyond the slope of the lawn, Margaret could see her brother, absorbed in the task of tying back some overgrown ramblers.

It was as good a time as any to tell John, she assured herself and, gathering what resolution she could, she went out into the garden.

As she crossed the lawn, however, he stopped what he was doing and watched her coming with such obvious interest and affectionate curiosity that she was not entirely surprised when he greeted her with:

"Hello, Meg! What's this about you and Giles getting yourselves engaged?"

She laughed, and tried to look reasonably happy and confused.

"How did you know?" she asked.

"Giles told me, not half an hour ago."

She was immediately divided between relief at not having to make her own explanations and faint resentment that anyone else should usurp her privilege of telling John herself. So that, instead of asking—as any really engaged girl would have done—where her beloved now was, she inquired, rather anxiously:

"What do you—think about it, John?"

"My dear, if you're happy, I'm delighted, of course," her brother replied promptly. "Giles is a very good fellow, it seems to me. And if you two marry, it will give you a home of your own again, and take him out of Eileen's too possessive clutches."

Margaret made no comment on that. Instead, she found herself asking, not quite wisely perhaps:

"You don't find it all rather—sudden—and odd?"

"I suppose these things are often sudden, Meg." John smiled, in a unusually meditative way. "What was it? Love at first sight?"

"Certainly not!" replied his sister, so emphatically that he laughed and raised his eyebrows, and she felt bound to add, more mildly, "If you remember, none of us was particularly pleased about his coming at first."

"That's true. But these things do happen, Meg."

"What things?" It was Margaret's turn to look surprised.

"The sudden, inescapable discovery that you've met the one person who is going to matter most in your life."

"Well—yes, I suppose it happens that way sometimes," Margaret agreed. But she looked inquiringly at her brother, for she had never heard him talk like this before, and she wondered if he had some idea that he *ought* to say something of the kind to his newly engaged sister.

One glance at him, however, was enough to show her that whatever he had said came from inner conviction rather than any desire to please. And, forgetting her own affairs for the moment, she exclaimed impulsively:

"Why, John, what makes you say that, I wonder? You said it almost as though it were a—a recent and personal experience."

"Clever little Meg!" He laughed and flushed very slightly. "That's just what it is. A recent and personal experience." And he glanced down at a sprig of leaves that he was holding and twirled it a little self-consciously in his fingers.

"John, do you mean that you—that you too——" for she must remember to keep herself convincingly in the picture—"have found someone who——"

"Oh, no, my dear!" He laughed and looked up again. "It's nothing as beautifully cut and dried as your arrangement." Little did he know! "There's no question of an engagement. I hardly know her. I suppose it sounds mad to you. I don't know why I'm telling you—except that, in your present mood, you'll probably understand better than most."

He paused, but she offered no comment on her romantic mood of the moment. And then she said softly, "Tell me, then, John."

"There's remarkably little to tell," he confessed. "She stopped off at the gardens yesterday, in a little red two-seater she was driving. She wanted some flowers—armfuls of them because she was happy, she said." He smiled at the recollection and, astounded, Margaret realized that she had never seen her brother look like that before.

"She came with me while I cut them, and asked me all sorts of questions—genuinely interested questions—about the place. She was so gay and sparkling, and yet so sympathetic and understanding. It's no good, Meg—I just can't describe her, except to say that I suddenly knew that she was *my* girl. I suppose that's what is meant by falling in love at first sight."

"I suppose—it is," agreed Margaret. And suddenly she was heartbreakingly aware that, while her brother had found the real thing, she was playing out some absurd sort of charade with a mockery of it.

"Dear John——" her voice was not quite steady, though it was unusually tender—"it must have been a lovely experience."

"It was."

"But don't you know who she is?—don't you even know her name?"

"Oh, yes, of course!" He laughed. "I wasn't too far gone to find out that practical detail. She's one of the Grahams of Fernwood Grange. The only girl, I think. Her name's Hester."

CHAPTER V

"Hester Graham? Of—of Fernwood Grange?" stammered Margaret, in the utmost dismay. "Oh, John, it can't be!"

"Why not?" He was taken aback, but not really shaken by her protest.

"Because—oh, I'm sorry, I'm afraid this will hurt you terribly, but—she's just got engaged. To Paul Freemantle."

John did pale rather at that. But, to her boundless astonishment, he merely said:

"Well then, she's made a mistake. She's taken the wrong man. She must get out of the engagement."

"Get out of the engagement!" Margaret almost literally fell back from him. "You can't talk like that. She's engaged, I tell you. She's going to marry him. Whatever you feel about her, she's made her choice and——"

"She hadn't met me when she did that."

"John dear, I know that's how one feels——" Hadn't she felt the very same way herself?—"But there are things that one has to accept. She has got engaged to Paul Freemantle. Presumably she loves him——"

"There's no absolute presumption of that," John interrupted curtly. "People become engaged for all sorts of reasons—frequently because they're mistaken about their own feelings. She's mistaken, that's all. We're meant for each other—I know we are. *And she knew it too, Meg, before she left.*"

"Are you mad?" Margaret stared at her brother as though she had never really seen him before, which was rather how she felt at the moment. What frightened and astounded her more than anything else was his absolute calm as he made these outrageous statements. He spoke like someone who had learned a lesson and could not be persuaded to depart one iota from it.

"All right." He was not even annoyed by her passionate protest. "It can seem only madness to you, I see. Perhaps that's the way it would seem to anyone. Only—I know, I tell you. And she knows it too."

"How," asked Margaret, in a sort of fascination, "can you be sure of that? Did she say anything, do anything?"

"She—looked at me as she took the flowers, and neither of us said anything for almost half a minute, I guess. Then I asked her her name, and she just whispered it. She seemed half scared, and she said suddenly that she must go. I asked if she'd be coming back and at first she said, 'No.' And then she said, 'Yes, of course. I—have to, don't I?' And she went away, leaving me dumbstruck, only smiling in a way that I suppose anyone would call daft."

"But aren't you jumping to conclusions?" Margaret was deeply troubled. "There could have been other explanations for what she said, surely?"

"What other explanation?"

"I don't know. Only words are so easily misunderstood." She had herself discovered the truth of *that*, all too well!

"I understood her all right," John insisted obstinately. "And she understood me. I can only tell you that, Meg. She's the girl I love, and she's the girl I'm going to marry."

"But, even if she were not already engaged, I don't think the Grahams would consider you a match for her. They're wealthy people, John."

"So were Mother's people when Father married her," retorted John, looking oddly like his father at that moment. "No one thought that *they* would marry. But he got her, and they were happy all the years they had together."

"And what about Paul Freemantle?" She could hardly

believe that she was carrying a torch for Paul over his engagement to Hester.

"What about him?" asked her brother, with monumental indifference.

"Hasn't he got his rights too? He—I suppose he also loves Hester, and thinks she is the girl for him."

"Then he's mistaken," replied John. And suddenly Margaret realized that they were arguing in circles and merely coming round to the same obstinately held conviction.

She stopped, nonplussed. And at that her brother laughed and, giving her an affectionate hug, exclaimed:

"I shouldn't have intruded my mad hopes on your happiness just now. I'm terribly glad for you, Meg dear, if you've found the man you love. Be happy with your Giles, and leave me to work out my own love story. I'll manage, make no mistake."

And if he did? If, by some incredible, inexplicable chance, this mad conviction of his were correct, what then? *Had* he and Hester Graham really fallen in love with each other, almost at a glance? Did these things ever really happen, outside the pages of a book?

If so, and Hester had the strength and resolution to break through all the conventional ties of family and engagement—then Paul would be free once more. Bruised and shaken perhaps, but all the more in need of comfort for that. And who more willing to give that comfort than Margaret? She understood him as no other girl did. She could forgive him willingly for what would become a temporary disaffection. They could take up their love story where they left off——

Suddenly, with a sensation bordering on panic, she remembered her own engagement. In the eyes of Paul, and the world, *she* was not free. She was an engaged girl. Unless she could change all that, she was just the person to whom Paul would *not* turn for consolation.

"I—I must find Giles," she murmured confusedly.

And John, smiling understandingly at her absorption in her own affairs, said, "He went towards the river. He said it was the ideal morning for an engaged man to take a walk and reflect on his happiness."

He over-does it, she thought impatiently. But she left her brother, with a slightly strained smile, and took the path towards the river.

"Anyway, the whole thing is absurd—unbelievable," she told herself presently. "John's just got one of those crazy ideas that we all get from time to time. Usually we don't confide them to anyone, and they presently die a natural death. One can't just fall headlong in love with some other man's girl, on the very day she announces her engagement. Or even if, inconceivably, that happens, *she* doesn't do the same thing. Hester's in love with Paul. Why else did she get engaged to him? Unless, of course, he just swept her off her feet——"

Margaret bit her lip as she recalled, all too clearly, Paul's irresistible way of sweeping one off one's feet.

And then, before she could follow that disturbing thought further, she met Giles coming back from his morning walk, and he greeted her with a casual friendliness which struck a very nice balance between the step-brother he was and the devoted suitor he was supposed to be.

Together they strolled back to the house—to face breakfast and any further family comment.

Penelope, now brought up to date with the state of the engagement, was a little reproachful about having been misled the previous evening.

"I think you might have been less cagey yesterday, when Dorothy and I and Mrs. Emms asked you about things," she said. "You as good as said there was nothing in it—and *now* what am I to tell them?"

"Do you have to tell them anything?" inquired Margaret. A question which Penelope ignored, with the disdain it deserved.

"I shall have to say that you wanted to keep it quiet until you'd told Father," she decided.

"And me too, I hope." Eileen smiled with rather synthetic playfulness. "I'm a parent too, you know, Penelope. My feelings also deserve a *little* consideration, don't you think?"

"Oh, yes, I daresay." Penelope was cheerfully indifferent about her stepmother's sensitive feelings. "But, in a way, a girl has to ask her parents' permission, doesn't she? Giles doesn't have to ask yours."

This crude statement of the case produced an awkward silence. Then Eileen said she thought Penelope was allowed to talk altogether too much about the affairs of her elders, and wasn't there something to be said for little girls being seen and not heard?

As none of them could imagine this admirable dictum ever applying very strictly to Penelope, there was silence again, until Mr. Masters turned to Margaret and Giles with an indulgent air and said:

"Well, I suppose you two want to go off on your own for the day?" Eileen made a quick movement of her hand, but he either did not notice this or ignored it, for he went on, "You had better make the most of the weekend. You won't have much time for each other during the week. An engagement's all very well, but I can't have it disrupting work, you know."

Both murmured that they understood this, though Margaret had difficulty in concealing her reluctance to spend the whole day in Giles's company—pretending to be a devoted fiancée when people were by, and wondering what to talk about when they were not.

Giles, however, managed much better. He said, with quite a show of enthusiasm, that a day out together would be wonderful.

"We'll take the car, and just drive wherever the fancy takes us, shall we, darling?" And darling managed to smile convincingly and say that would be delightful.

Eileen looked anything but pleased at once more being

frustrated in any plan she might have for a quiet—and possibly damaging—talk with Giles. But even she could not raise any open objection to a plan so desirable for an engaged couple. And so, presently, Margaret found herself once more in the car beside Giles, with the soft April air blowing in through the open window.

"We're going to get to know an awful lot of the countryside, if we're expected to do this every weekend," she remarked, rather ruefully, as they drove along.

But he laughed and said:

"They'll soon get used to the situation and your father won't be so eager to make plans for us. Meanwhile, I suggest you and I take this opportunity of going to see Maxine today."

"Oh, yes, do let's!" Margaret was quite enchanted with this diversion. "But do you think she'll mind our coming without any warning, like this?"

"We shan't be coming without any warning," Giles assured her. "I telephoned to Maxine this morning, from the call-box down the road, and suggested that you and I should lunch on the way and arrive at her place about three."

"I—see." Margaret gave him a faintly disturbed glance, which he appeared not to notice. "How did you— describe me, Giles? I mean—did you explain about our— our odd situation?"

"I told her we were engaged, if that's what you mean."

"Oh, did you have to do that?" There was a note of protest in Margaret's voice.

"What else?" He seemed genuinely surprised. "You can't be my fiancée to one set of people and not to another, you know."

"But she's not in any contact with the family," Margaret objected. "Surely, with her at least we could be ourselves?"

"Too risky," he declared. "We've seen already what complications it can cause if we tell one person one thing, and someone else nothing. Suppose—as I can't help hoping—Maxine decides to make some sort of overture to Mother?"

"Well, wouldn't *that* be the moment to put her in the picture?"

"It might be too late. She might telephone, on the spur of the moment, and if she and Mother talked about us at cross-purposes, we'd be presented with another crisis. No, no, Meg, the only way is to play our roles thoroughly, for all and sundry—however free from danger the situation may seem. Then, when we decide we've kept it up long enough, we can break the engagement in the usual way—and no one need be any the wiser."

"How soon do you think we can break it?" Margaret asked, her thoughts very much on the strange situation which might, or might not, have arisen over Hester Graham.

"Don't sound so unflatteringly eager," Giles admonished her. "Am I *so* trying in the role of fiancé?"

"No." Margaret's laugh was genuinely contrite. "As a matter of fact, you could hardly do it better. Only——" she sighed slightly—"I don't think a false position comes very easily to me."

"I must be more devious by nature than you are," he said. "I'm rather enjoying this."

"Oh, Giles, you're not!—Are you, really?"

"Since it gives me so much of your charming company, you don't expect me to say I'm not enjoying it, do you?" he retorted.

"I should have thought you'd hate it," she said frankly.

"Well, I don't," was the unexpectedly curt reply. And after that they drove in silence for some while.

They lunched in Newcastle, which reminded Margaret suddenly that Elinor was still in complete ignorance of all that had happened.

"I ought to see Elinor," she told Giles. "There isn't time now, I know. But perhaps on the way back——" She stopped, recollecting that, with her elder sister, she would want a heart-to-heart talk. Not at all the kind of talk she could have in front of Giles.

Perhaps he realized the thought behind the pause, because he said, quite amiably:

"I suppose you girls will want a chat on your own. I could drop you on the way back and fetch you later."

"Oh, no, I couldn't bring you right into Newcastle again," she protested. "Why don't we arrange it differently? Suppose I leave your sister's place earlier than you. I can take the bus from Morpeth into Newcastle. There are plenty of them and it doesn't take long. Then you can fetch me an hour or two later, on your way back. How would that do?"

He said it would do very well, and she thought he was not sorry to have some time alone with Maxine. Probably they had nearly as much to say to each other as she and Elinor would have. Possibly even, when he was alone with her, he would choose to tell Maxine the truth.

And, even as she thought this, he said reflectively:

"If you very much prefer Maxine to know the real position between us, it's up to you, of course. She is good at keeping her own counsel, I might say."

"I'll see how the position develops," Margaret replied. And by that she really meant, of course, that she would have to see what sort of a person Maxine was before she entrusted the whole story to her.

Morpeth—that most charming of market towns—was drowsing in the sunshine of a quiet Sunday afternoon when they passed through it and drove a couple of miles further on, to the home of Maxine and her family.

Margaret was not very sure what she had expected. But she gave an involuntary exclamation of surprise and pleasure as they drove up to the compact little stone house, with its colourful, if rather untidy, flower-garden in front, and somewhat straggling outhouses behind.

It was not quite important enough to rank as a farm. But there was the contented clucking of hens somewhere in the back, while a couple of cows in the field beyond, and the unmistakable outlines of hives in the middle distance, suggested that Maxine and her husband pursued a variety of country interests.

Even before the car stopped, the front door of the house was thrown open and a girl uncommonly reminiscent of Eileen came running down the path.

In colouring—even in her basic elegance of figure—she was almost disconcertingly like her mother. But there the likeness ended. For Maxine Ritherdon radiated a warmth and sincerity that Eileen could not have achieved in a hundred years. Her eyes sparkled with humour and good feeling, her mouth lifted at the corners in the frankest of smiles. And, if the hands she held out in a welcoming gesture were a little work-worn, and her dress was one in which her mother would not have been seen dead, she seemed to Margaret, in that first moment, one of the liveliest and most vital people she had ever seen.

"Giles, you angel, to bring her the very first day!"

Maxine embraced her brother with uninhibited warmth, and then kissed Margaret with as little lack of ceremony.

"Dear, I hadn't even got used to thinking of you as a stepsister before Giles informed me you were also the girl he is going to marry," she declared. "It's all too exciting. Come in, come in! The children are dying to see you. Susan and Don have never had a real auntie before, and they're very curious about you."

While she was talking, she had shepherded them up the garden path and into the house where, in an unexpectedly large and comfortable living-room, they found Bernard and the children.

Nothing about the place would have been acceptable by Eileen's standards, and the pleasant, heavily built man who lifted Susan off his knee and rose to greet them was a homely rather than an elegant figure. But a sort of solid, comforting happiness radiated from both Maxine and her husband. And, although the children came forward shyly, it was obvious that, quite naturally, they expected a loving welcome.

Seated in one of the shabby armchairs, Margaret found herself an object of intense interest to both the eight-year-old Susan and the six-year-old Don, and very soon she was telling them about Penelope, and answering their eager questions. This gave Giles an opportunity to talk to his sister, and, in between the artless conversation which Susan and Don conducted with her, Margaret could not help hearing something of the half amused, half rueful exchange of news about Eileen.

It was not until Bernard took Giles off to see some new enterprise on his small piece of land that the two girls had a chance to talk with any intimacy. And then, before Margaret could even decide whether or not she intended to tell Maxine the true situation, the older girl exclaimed:

"I'm so *glad* about you and Giles!"

"Are you?" Margaret was faintly uncomfortable at having provoked such genuine delight by false means. "Why, I wonder?"

"You're just what he needs." Maxine stated that simply and positively. "You're too sensible to have many illusions about Mother and so—though I don't want to sound an entirely undutiful daughter—you must know she's as self-centred as the hub of a wheel. That makes her madly possessive, and it's only because he's basically a very determined person that Giles has managed not to be swallowed up. I was always nervous in case—in a wild bid for independence—he'd marry the wrong sort of girl. Now I see he's not going to, and I'm more happy and relieved than I can say."

"But you don't really know what sort of girl I am yet." Margaret spoke protestingly, though she smiled.

"I can make a very good guess." Maxine gave her such a shrewd glance that Margaret was more than ever aware that she was there on false pretences, and blushed.

That made Maxine laugh, and she added warmly:

"I'm specially glad about you and Giles because he's such a dear person. He *deserves* to have someone nice."

"I'm sure he does," agreed Margaret, earnestly. And she opened her mouth to add that, in fact, he deserved someone much nicer than herself and that he would soon be free to choose again.

But, before she could snatch at this not very good opportunity, Maxine went on:

"He won't have told you himself, of course, but he's been an angel to Bernard and me. We had a terribly tough time in the early days. That's one reason why we didn't have the children until we'd been married some years. But, as soon as Giles was old enough to handle his own money, he insisted on helping us to get a place of our own. I don't think Mother even knew about it. And, with just that bit of help, we changed our luck—and here we are!"

She smiled and made a quick, comprehensive gesture with her hands, which seemed to take in, with loving pride and gratitude, not only the shabby room itself, but the children and the indefinable glow of happiness which was so much part of the place.

"I'm so glad." Margaret was moved, to a degree she would not have thought possible. "And I'm sure Giles is all you say. I—I hope he'll be very happy. But, as a matter of fact——"

"Oh, my dear, of course he will be! It's written all over him," Maxine declared. "You mustn't be so diffident about yourself. You're absolutely the person to make him happy. I know it!—I can feel it in my bones. And my bones are remarkably reliable in these matters," she added, with a laugh.

She was so certain about this, and so happy in her own certainty, that Margaret simply could not find the right moment, after that, to explain that it was all make-believe. And, when the two men came back, she managed to whisper to Giles:

"Don't tell her, after all. She's so—so terribly happy about it all. We'll find a better time, when it won't come as quite such a blow."

He did raise his eyebrows and give a quizzical look at that. But all he said was:

"Very well. I leave the timing to you."

The rest of the visit passed all too quickly, and it was obvious that Maxine was genuinely reluctant to let Margaret go. But she understood immediately about the necessity of the two sisters having a heart-to-heart talk, particularly in view of the recent engagement. So she kissed Margaret affectionately, begged her to come again soon, and let Giles drive her down to the Market Place, where she was to get her Newcastle bus.

It was a short drive. But he found time to ask, curiously:

"What made you so sure that Maxine should not be told?"

"Oh, it would have been like a slap in the face, on a day when she's so artlessly happy," Margaret declared. "She's quite inexplicably pleased about it all. Convinced that—that marriage is just the right thing for you and that, for some reason or other, I'm the ideal person. I hadn't the heart to laugh."

"I should hope not! And what's so funny about it, anyway?"

"Well——" she was rather taken aback—"the idea of our being specially suited when, in actual fact, we couldn't have been more clumsily pushed into the arrangement."

He said nothing to that, possibly because he was at that moment negotiating an awkward corner. But as they drew up near the bus stand, he observed:

"We might not be any the less suited for having been forced into this arrangement. We just haven't had a chance to find out, one way or the other."

"Oh, Giles, don't be absurd——" she began.

But her bus came in just then, and he leaned over to open the car door for her.

"Run along," he admonished her briskly. "You'll be just in time."

So she jumped out, called goodbye to him and ran for her bus, with the odd feeling that she had left an important conversation unfinished.

Once she was in the bus, and they were driving out of the town—past the beautiful slope of the public gardens which are, justifiably, the pride of Morpeth—she thought back over the last exchange of words between herself and Giles.

What on earth did he mean by saying they were not necessarily any the less suited for having been forced into the present arrangement? Was it simply one of those provocative remarks that men liked to throw off, just for the sake of argument, or was he hinting that he found the present situation rather less absurd and impossible than she did?

He couldn't have meant that! Margaret told herself that she just could not take any more complications in her relationship with Giles. He simply *had* to keep to his passive role of pretended fiancé. Even more so now that a faint, absurd hope kept on thrusting its way in, in view of John's unexpected revelation.

Not of course that one must attach any real importance to what John said, she assured herself—while all the time attaching immense importance to it, of course. After all, the plain fact was that Paul was engaged to Hester, and no amount of wishful thinking was going to alter that. And yet—if Hester did completely change her mind —if John's extraordinary fixation were somehow correct——

Margaret stared out at the busy road, unseeing. And not until they passed through Gosforth, and she knew she was nearing her stop, did she wrench her mind away from agitating but golden reflections and concentrate on what she was going to tell Elinor.

When she finally arrived at the flat, she found that, by great good luck, Elinor was in but that her fellow tenant, Dulcie, was out. And, from the warmth of the welcome which her sister bestowed upon her, Margaret guessed that

Elinor's satisfaction with her new life had not prevented her from missing her family badly.

"Meg, how wonderful to see you!" She hugged Margaret with unusual fervour. "I was just feeling a bit—well, not *blue*, exactly—but lonesome enough to dislike my own company."

"I know." Margaret nodded understandingly, as she dropped into a comfortable chair and regarded her sister with affection.

It struck her that Elinor looked oddly young, and somehow a little defenceless, shorn of her home background and not yet completely established in her self-chosen one. And, as she cried, "Now tell me everything!" Margaret suddenly saw her again as a schoolgirl, in the days when they used to share all their secrets.

Perhaps it was that curious impression, or perhaps it was the irresistible luxury of being pressed to indulge in complete frankness at last, after so much unfamiliar concealment, that suddenly loosened Margaret's tongue. At any rate, whatever the reason, there swept over her that wonderful sensation of release which probably occurs only between sisters and, with a great sigh of relief, she exclaimed :

"Oh, Elinor, what a wonderful thought! That's just what I'm going to do—tell you the lot! And, to begin with, I've somehow got myself engaged to Giles."

"Meg!" Elinor was aghast. "You can't have! He's *against* us; in the enemy camp, as you might say."

That shook Margaret slightly, for she had long ago given up regarding Giles in that light. But, without pausing to explain this significant fact, she laughed and said quickly :

"Don't get excited. It's not a genuine engagement. It's——"

"Not a genuine engagement?" Elinor seemed to find that even more staggering than the previous statement. "Meg, what on earth have you been up to? I shouldn't have left you on your own!" she cried, in sudden remorse.

"Yes, you should, if that was what you wanted to do," Margaret assured her promptly. "Your going had nothing to do with it, so don't worry. It's a long story, and you're the only one to hear it complete. But you must promise never, never to tell anyone else."

"Cross my heart!" Elinor, both anxious and intrigued, hastily made the sign which had been current between them in their schooldays.

Aware that she could not explain the pretended engagement to Giles without admitting to being previously involved with Paul, Margaret resolutely gave the story of this first. At which Elinor, intent on every word she was uttering, murmured unexpectedly, "So the rumours were true."

"What rumours?" Margaret asked sharply.

"After I came here, and got in with a very varied crowd, I heard people say that Paul Freemantle had been more or less engaged to a girl in Cromburgh," Elinor said slowly. "Dulcie told me that your name had been mentioned. And, though I assured her there was nothing in it, I did wonder, Meg. There were times, a month or two back, when you were obviously living in a world of your own. I thought, even then, that you might have met someone who meant a lot to you. And then—you were the least shaken of us all, you know, when Father married. You took the news so calmly that it did occur to me you might be finding it a blessing in disguise; an opportunity to shelve some of the family commitments and follow a life of your own."

"You noticed so much?" Margaret gave an incredulous, half vexed little laugh. "I thought I hid my feelings better."

"You hid them very well," Elinor told her. "And I only wondered. I didn't *know*. It's just that I'm not entirely surprised by what you're telling me. But go on. How come you confided in Giles Ormby, of all people?"

Margaret explained how Giles had been the first to give her the news of Paul's engagement and how, in her

4

distress, she simply could not hide what significance this
had for her. Then she went on to describe the events of the
previous day, when everything she did and said seemed
to involve her more and more deeply in a false position.

"You should never have *started* such a thing!" remon-
strated Elinor.

"What would you have done?" retorted Margaret.
"Allowed Paul to realize just how sick and humiliated you
felt because of his desertion?"

"N—no, not that," Elinor conceded. "But I don't
think I could have accepted rescue from Giles."

"I shouldn't have thought I could either," Margaret
assured her. "But when one gets pushed from one crisis
to another there's no time to find an ideal solution, Elinor.
One just improvises and hopes for the best. What started
as a mild face-saver in front of Paul developed into a full-
scale situation, almost before I knew what was happening."

"I think Giles took advantage of your bad luck,"
declared Elinor resentfully.

"Oh, Elinor, he didn't! Why on earth should he, anyway? He had nothing to gain from this ridiculous mock-
engagement."

"It could be his way of cadging favour with at least one
member of the family."

"No, no, it's not like that at all," Margaret insisted.
"He genuinely wanted to help me—and he has."

"Well—it could be." Elinor sounded sceptical. "But
what is the position now? I can't see that you've gained
anything. The man you really want is securely tied up to
another girl, while——"

"Not—so securely," Margaret interrupted, though
hesitantly because she was not sure that she should tell
John's secret as well as her own.

"What do you mean by that, exactly?" Elinor's eyes
widened again.

"It's not really my secret this time, Elinor," Margaret
admitted. "Though I suppose, if you'd been on the spot,

John would have been more likely to tell you than me."

"John!" Elinor interrupted in her turn. "Do you mean to say that *John* is in this too?"

"In a way, yes. He's—well, he's fallen in love with Hester Graham," Margaret said, since there seemed no need to state this other than bluntly.

"I don't believe it!" Elinor thrust her hands through her hair, in a gesture of agitated unbelief, as though she thought this might help her to understand better the extraordinary behaviour of her family since she had left them to their own devices. "I don't know what's come over you all. You'll be telling me next that Penelope has started a love-life of her own."

Margaret laughed at this and was at least able to reassure her sister on that score.

"But why Hester Graham?" cried Elinor.

"I don't know," Margaret admitted. "It seems she called in one day at the nurseries—good heavens, I suppose it was only yesterday! though this crazy business seems to have been going on for days. She wanted to buy some flowers, and John went with her, to cut them for her. Isn't it the most extraordinary coincidence that, of all places, she should call in at John's place, when——"

"No." Suddenly Elinor uncurled her legs, which had been tucked up comfortably under her, and sat up very straight. "No, that wasn't coincidence, Meg. That was intention, if you ask me."

"What do you mean?" Margaret looked puzzled.

"Why, you don't suppose I was the only person to hear those rumours about you and Paul, do you? Hester probably heard them too. She must have seen our name over the entrance to the nurseries often enough, as she drove through Cromburgh on her way to and from Newcastle. My guess is that she suddenly decided to go in and see what she could find out for herself."

"On the very day her engagement was announced?" objected Margaret.

"Perhaps that was the day when she simply *had* to make sure," Elinor countered.

"But I wasn't even there. I never am."

"She wasn't to know that. For all she knew, John's devoted sister was his chief assistant. Given a little luck, she might well have had the opportunity to exchange a few words with or about the girl her Paul was supposed to have let down."

"From John's account, my name wasn't even mentioned." Margaret still looked doubtful. "They didn't talk about *me*, Elinor."

"What did they talk about?"

"John's hopes and plans and—themselves. According to him, it was a sort of instantaneous recognition of each other. Though he'd never seen her before——"

"That isn't quite right, you know," Elinor interrupted suddenly. "He did see her once, at that big fancy-dress do at the Town Hall last October. She came as a Dresden shepherdess or something rather corny like that—though I'm bound to say she looked lovely. Her party arrived very late—they'd come on from something else, I guess—and we left soon after. But I remember John being very struck then. He asked me who she was, but I didn't know at the time. It was only later that I found out, and by then I didn't think of him as being sufficiently interested for me to mention it."

"Well, he could hardly be more interested," Margaret observed dryly. "He simply brushed aside my information that she was already engaged. He's convinced that it was more or less love at first sight for both of them. And though I know it all sounds improbable and idiotic as I'm telling you now, he's so utterly and absolutely certain that it's simply impossible to insist that he's wrong."

"I know what you mean. He has these extraordinary flashes sometimes," said John's twin knowledgeably. "And the funny thing is that he's nearly always right."

CHAPTER VI

For quite a few seconds Margaret stared thoughtfully at her sister. Then she said, almost as though she hardly dared to voice the words:

"You think John might be *right*, about himself and Hester? You think it's not impossible that they fell head-long in love, even though she'd just got engaged to Paul?"

Elinor shrugged.

"Nothing's impossible, Meg. There's nowt so queer as folk, as they say. I'm not saying that it is so. I'm merely saying that John has an uncanny habit of being right when he gets these odd hunches."

"But, if he *were* right—and Hester admitted her true feelings too and broke her engagement, and the Grahams agreed to her marrying John——"

"Which is assuming a lot, of course," Elinor pointed out.

"I know. But suppose all that did happen, then Paul would be free again."

"Undoubtedly. But what then?"

"Oh, Elinor, do you suppose I've thought of much else all day?" cried Margaret. "All this silly business with Giles is nothing beside the fact that Paul——"

A sharp ring at the front-door bell brought her to an abrupt stop, and Elinor exclaimed in surprise, "Who's that, I wonder? Dulcie has her key."

"I think," said Margaret, sounding faintly apologetic, to her own surprise, "I think it's probably Giles, come to fetch me."

"Giles?" Elinor sounded annoyed. Then she added impatiently, "Oh dear, yes, of course. If you're sort of engaged to him, I suppose he has a right to squire you around. I'd better let him in." And, rather reluctantly, she went to open the front door.

Margaret heard them greeting each other with studied politeness but no warmth, and a moment later Elinor came back into the room, accompanied by Giles.

"Here's your so-called fiancé, come to collect you," she observed, in a tone that was less than friendly. And, as Giles raised his eyebrows, Margaret explained hastily :

"I've told Elinor the true story. There seemed no reason to do anything else."

"I should think not, indeed!" Elinor sounded annoyed at the mere idea that she might have been fobbed off with a tale. "I think it's a pity you ever got involved in this business——" she spoke directly to Giles—"and the sooner you get out of it, the better."

"Timing is important in all great enterprises," Giles assured her, a trifle maliciously, and Margaret could pretty well see the sparks flying between him and Elinor. "We shall have to find the right moment, you know. Just now the whole family is intrigued by romance in its midst, and we can't snatch that satisfaction away from them, just as they're enjoying themselves. Even if we wanted to," he added thoughtfully, in a tone which reminded Margaret uncomfortably of his saying they were not necessarily unsuited, just because they had been thrust together.

Elinor too seemed to find that last remark provocative, for she said impatiently :

"Of course I know you can't get disengaged on the day after you've announced your engagement. But I should imagine it's a position you'd like to have resolved as soon as possible. It must be embarrassing for you both."

"I'm not in the least embarrassed," Giles assured her mildly. "How about you, Meg?"

Margaret sensed, rather than heard, the catch of Elinor's breath as Giles so easily used her family pet name.

"Oh, I—I'm not embarrassed exactly," she said

hastily. "It's all rather awkward, of course. But I can't pretend I'm not grateful for the—the original effort on my behalf. Anyway, I'm afraid we must go now, Elinor dear."

Elinor raised no objection, since obviously she and Margaret could not continue their conversation with any degree of intimacy now that Giles had arrived. So she kissed Margaret goodbye. But, as she did so, she managed to whisper:

"Don't count too much on the Hester-John business. But I'll keep my ear to the ground, and let you know if I hear any news or gossip."

Then Giles and Margaret went on their way, driving for quite a while in silence until Giles observed, thoughtfully rather than regretfully:

"I'm afraid Elinor doesn't like me much."

"Oh, you mustn't take her sharp way of speaking too much to heart! She was rather put out by our news, of course, but——"

"Don't worry. I shan't be lying awake at night about it," Giles assured her dryly. "I was merely making conversation. And I was going to add that I think my sister likes you a great deal more than your sister likes me."

"Oh——" Margaret had an obscure sort of feeling that she ought to be indignant on Elinor's behalf, but she was also aware of most genuine pleasure that Maxine should have approved of herself. And she ended by saying diplomatically, "I'm very glad if Maxine liked me. I liked her immensely. Tell me, did you manage to discuss the possibility of any—any sort of approach between her and Eileen?"

"Oh, yes. She's not at all averse to it, now that we're all living within reasonable distance of each other. But I think she finds it difficult to take my efforts seriously. She declares that nothing will make Mother show an interest in her again."

"And do you think anything will?"

"At least I shall try."

"How?" inquired Margaret, with genuine curiosity.

"I don't know, Meg. I think I shall just leave it to the inspiration of the moment. And perhaps you'll back me up, when the time comes?"

"*I?*" Margaret was rather startled at the idea of being personally involved in this intimate family affair. "But I don't think Eileen would be inclined to pay much attention to anything I said, Giles."

"Not if you made a direct argument of it, I agree. But she's rather—competitive, you know. If she found that you had seen and liked Maxine, I'm not at all sure that she wouldn't want at least to do as much as you had."

Margaret turned and stared at him.

"You do realize that makes her sound a pretty horrid person, don't you?" she said.

"You have to take people as they are, Meg. Not as you might wish them to be," he replied good-humouredly. "The fact that I can see Mother's little weaknesses doesn't alter my opinion that there's something wrong in a mother and daughter not seeing anything of each other. I still intend to go on with my efforts to bring them together, at least in a semblance of friendly feeling. And I'd appreciate it very much if you would weigh in on my side."

It was impossible, of course, to deny him that measure of support, in view of the way he had come to her rescue when she was in difficulties. So Margaret said, with as good a grace as she could, that she would certainly help in any way that seemed possible. Though she reserved to herself the cowardly hope that she would not be called on to do this for some while.

Hope proved to be vain, however. For, when they arrived home, it was to find Eileen sitting on her own in the drawing-room, a book lying disregarded in her lap, and on her face an expression of wistful resignation which Margaret felt morally certain she had assumed as soon as she heard the car draw up outside.

"Why, my dear!" (The endearment was strictly in the

singular, though she had to look at them both since they
came in together.) "Has it been a lovely day?" And she
smiled as though she would be the last to resent the
portion of unloved loneliness which they had thrust upon
her.

"Lovely, thank you." Even Giles sounded a trifle
brusque in the face of this martyred sweetness. "For you
too, I expect, if you took that drive beyond Hexham that
Robert and you were discussing this morning."

Eileen was not going to be side-tracked on to any
pleasant expedition of hers, however. She merely smiled
a trifle more wistfully and said:

"My thoughts were with you, darling, naturally.
Where did *you* go?"

Probably, thought Margaret, he had not expected to be
presented with an opening quite so quickly as this, and
she guessed that the second's pause was Giles's sole con-
cession to whatever nervousness he might feel. In an odd
way, she was glad, suddenly, that she was with him now
and that he had actually asked for her support. Because,
all at once, it was much easier for her than for him to say
calmly:

"We went to see Maxine. She and her husband have a
charming place, just beyond Morpeth."

"Maxine?" Eileen repeated the name almost in a
whisper, as though it came unfamiliarly to her tongue.
"Maxine! But I had no idea——"

She broke off, and Margaret noticed that her hands
were opening and closing, in a nervous movement suggestive of some powerful emotion only just suppressed.

"It was quite exciting, meeting a stepsister," Margaret
went on determinedly, in a tone so natural that she was
rather proud of herself. "I liked her on sight—and the
children are adorable. It's really not a long drive from
here, Eileen. You must get Giles to run you over one
evening, now that the days are getting so much longer."

And, having made this revolutionary suggestion with
all the air of one suggesting the obvious, Margaret caught

up her coat, smiled innocently at her stupefied stepmother, and went out of the room, leaving Giles to take
up the tale from there.

She knew that, in precipitating them straight into a
discussion of the situation, she had done Giles the best
service she could. It had been a bit like throwing a puppy
into the water and making it swim, she told herself with
a laugh, as she went upstairs, but at least it had saved
Giles the strain of taking the first plunge on his own. Now,
whatever he and his mother had to say to each other was
better said without an outsider present. For whichever
way the discussion went, Eileen was going to need a
certain amount of face-saving. And—as Margaret recognized without rancour—for this to happen in front of the
girl she already disliked would have been unbearable for
her.

Supper was usually a late-ish meal in the Masters household on a Sunday evening, and even when Margaret had
washed and changed, there was still a little time left. She
went down to the kitchen, to see if Gloria needed any help.
But, finding her services were not required, she went out
into the garden, in the half-confessed hope of finding her
brother there.

Not that she felt there was much to be added to their
conversation of the morning. But because John was the
key to the situation which caused her both anguish and
hope, he had an irresistible attraction for her at the
moment.

She found him, busy as usual, in the garden, for John
could never resist a job which needed doing where anything was growing. He straightened up immediately at
the sight of her, however, and inquired with a grin :

"Well, how's the engaged girl? Had a good day?"

"Lovely, thank you. What did you do?"

"I went over to see Hester."

He said it so calmly that it was a split-second before
Margaret took in the full significance of what he had said.
Then she gasped and exclaimed :

"You went to see Hester Graham? But whatever excuse could you give?"

"She left her powder compact on the side of the desk when she paid for her flowers yesterday," he said with a smile.

"Intentionally?" Margaret asked, before she could stop herself.

"I don't know." He was still smiling. "Perhaps. Anyway, it had to be returned, didn't it?"

"Yes," Margaret agreed, with her eyes on her brother's face. "And so—what happened?"

"I stayed to tea."

"Just with Hester?"

"No. Her parents were there. Mr. Graham knows Father a bit, in the way of business. And it seems that Mrs. Graham met Eileen once or twice in London."

"Yes, I know. They were there last night, as a matter of fact."

"So I discovered. I was made quite surprisingly welcome, Meg." He still seemed to be savouring that with pleasure. "Hester made me tell her father something of my plans—more of them than I really intended, now I come to think of it," he admitted, with a laugh. "But she—they talk the same language as I do. It's easy to slip into talking of one's ambitions there. I felt very much at home," he finished simply.

"Was—was Paul there?" Margaret made herself ask.

"Who?—Oh, Paul Freemantle. No, no." John dismissed him with a slight shake of the head, as being of very minor importance.

"Did no one even mention him?" inquired Margaret incredulously, for she felt very slightly incensed on Paul's behalf, absurd though this might be.

"Yes. I think Mrs. Graham said something about his not having been able to come because he had to fly to Paris on some journalistic assignment." Then he laughed and added almost mischievously, "Don't look so solemn, Meg. He wasn't really missed."

"I can't help looking solemn,".Margaret protested. "He's engaged to Hester. You can't just pretend he doesn't exist."

"No? Well, that's just what I did pretend," John retorted. "I can't take him seriously, Meg. I'm a little sorry for him, when I think about him at all, but I can't take him seriously."

"*She* took him sufficiently seriously to get engaged to him," Margaret pointed out.

"That's true," John agreed, but without appearing to give the fact much weight.

At that moment there was the sound of Penelope vigorously ringing the bell to indicate that supper was ready. But, as they turned towards the house, Margaret simply could not resist asking:

"Did you get any time *alone* with Hester, John?"

"Yes. She wanted to show me their garden. It's quite a big one. We strolled up to the end of it and back. And if you want to know if I told her I loved her—I didn't. At least, not in words. I might scare her if I rush her too much. But a lot can be said without words, Meg, as I daresay you and Giles have found out." And he laughed again.

"Giles and I? Oh—oh, yes," agreed Margaret, suddenly recalling her own engaged state. "But, John, don't attach too much significance to glances and handclasps, or whatever you indulged in. You could be riding for a frightful fall, my dear."

"I could be. But I'm not," John replied equably, as they re-entered the house. And Margaret had the conviction that, even if they had been able to prolong this conversation for another hour, they would have got no further than this.

It was both exhilarating and terribly disturbing.

Either John was right—and the possibility of her own happiness was dawning again. Or he was hopelessly wrong, and was going to have to meet a crushing disappointment.

Her thoughts were so completely on this one problem that she experienced something of a shock when they entered the dining-room and Penelope—evidently bursting with information—cried:

"John, has Margaret been telling you the news? Isn't it exciting?"

Margaret was petrified with alarm and astonishment. But John merely asked obligingly, "What news?"

"Why, about our stepsister, of course. Did you know that we've really got a stepsister? Giles has just been telling me. She's called Maxine and she lives not at all far away. Near Morpeth. And she's got two children, called Susan and Don, so they're really our niece and nephew. Goodness!" she suddenly clapped her hand to her mouth in rapturous astonishment. "I never thought! I've been an aunt for *years*, and never known it."

She was evidently entranced at the thought, and only slightly dashed when Giles pointed out that auntship could really only be considered to date from Eileen's marriage to her father.

"Oh—yes, that's a bit disappointing, isn't it?" Penelope said. "Still, they've *been* there all the time. And now you've actually seen them, haven't you, Meg? What are they like?"

"Very sweet and engaging," Margaret assured her, and she stole a glance at Eileen, to see how she was taking this spate of revelation.

The second Mrs. Masters was sitting, her head slightly bent, her expression grave and wistful, at the foot of the table, and her husband was sitting beside her, with his arm along the back of her chair, while he talked to her in an undertone.

"But are they dark or fair, fat or thin, or what?" Penelope wanted to know. "One doesn't have a full-grown niece and nephew every day. I think you might give us *some* details."

"Susan is dark and very bright-eyed, with straight hair and a fringe. She's what one means by cute. But Don has gorgeous copper-coloured hair and——" she glanced again at Eileen and said in some surprise—"I hadn't thought of it before, but Don is very much like you, Eileen."

"Is he, dear?" Eileen spoke in a sort of thoughts-too-deep-for-tears tone, but she shot a glance of dislike at Margaret.

Obviously, since Giles had put the talkative Penelope in possession of the facts, Eileen must have agreed to have the existence of Maxine recognized. But Margaret rather thought she was still in some doubt of the attitude she intended to take up with regard to this awkward addition to the family.

"Aren't you thrilled?" Penelope, blissfully insensitive to any emotional undercurrents, appealed to her step-mother with cheerful frankness. "He's your grandchild. Isn't that wonderful? It's wonderful finding you've got a niece and nephew, but it must be even *more* wonderful to have two grandchildren."

In spite of the thrice-repeated "wonderful" Eileen so obviously failed to share Penelope's feeling that even that enthusiast wilted a little. She made no further effort to excite Eileen's grandmotherly feelings. Instead, she turned to an even more fascinating riddle.

"I still don't understand why we didn't *know* anything about all this," she remarked. "Why should it have been a secret? And how is it that no one even saw our niece and nephew until this afternoon?"

"Pen, you talk too much," Margaret exclaimed warningly.

But suddenly inspiration seemed to have come to Eileen. For, looking up again, she smiled rather sadly and said:

"Not everyone's home life is as happy as yours, Penelope. I'm not blaming anyone. It isn't a mother's part to *blame*, even when she has been hurt. She must always try to understand. There was a time when my daughter didn't want to see me——"

"Why?" asked Penelope, with monumental simplicity.

"Dear, we're going to put a line under all that now." Eileen looked so forgiving that Margaret could not resist a glance at Giles, who was standing regarding the toes of his shoes with great attention.

He must have felt her eyes upon him, for he glanced up, and for a moment she saw a flicker of mingled resentment and amusement in his face. But he evidently felt that Eileen's determination to snatch the role of injured party was a reasonably small price to pay for a truce between mother and daughter, for he made no move to correct her as she went on :

"Everything is forgiven and forgotten now, so far as I am concerned. It's been a long, weary wait—but it's over, and so I'm going to forget all about it."

"Very generous of you, my dear," declared her husband, and he cleared his throat and looked genuinely moved.

"No, dear. That's just the way I *am*," Eileen assured him, as she put her hand on his. "I can't take any credit for it."

"Is that the way Maxine is too?" inquired Penelope, with irrepressible curiosity.

"Maxine is generosity itself," said Giles, quietly and unexpectedly. And there was a note in his voice which must have warned even Eileen not to query that, for she made no comment on this defence of her daughter. Instead, she smiled bravely round on everyone and said :

"Well, suppose we have supper now. It's been a very tiring and emotional sort of day. I suggest we leave this——" there was a slight catch in her voice—"this family matter to settle itself now."

With the notable exception of Penelope, everyone seemed willing to co-operate. And even Penelope was reduced to an occasional mutter about her niece and nephew, particularly when Margaret promised in a whisper to tell her more about them later.

The next day, back in the now familiar office at the

Works, Margaret found it hard to credit all that had happened since she had left on Friday evening. The other girls were exchanging comments on their weekend activities, and seemed to think they had crowded in a satisfactory amount of pleasure and excitement. But when one of them asked Margaret what she had done, the only answer she could produce was :

"Oh, I drove to the coast for dinner on Saturday evening, and yesterday I visited a friend near Morpeth."

No one seemed to find this wildly exciting and, to her relief, conversation drifted away from her again. Not that she could flatter herself that the news of her so-called engagement would remain secret long. Quite apart from the local gossip, which was doubtless already considerable, her father was now sufficiently pleased with the situation to make it a matter of comment. But, in her present mood, she felt more inclined to let events overtake her than to rush to meet them. When the other girls found out that she was engaged to Giles, she would admit the fact and smile. But she was certainly not going to provoke an outburst of interested comment and query before it was necessary.

She worked hard during the day, and even stayed late to finish something, rejecting her usual lift home in the family car in favour of a later bus which she could catch outside the gates.

All the other girls had gone, and even Miss Brant had cleared her desk and taken her departure, when the office door opened and, to her surprise, Giles came in.

"Hello. I thought you left early this afternoon," Margaret said. "Weren't you going into Newcastle?"

"I've been." He sat down on the side of Miss Brant's desk and smiled at her. "But when I got home, and your father told me you were working late, I thought I'd come and fetch you."

"That's very nice of you. Though I really could have caught the bus," Margaret told him. "I shan't be more than five minutes."

She began to type again, though it was a little difficult to keep her attention entirely on her work with him there. It had been kind of him to come, of course—but did he really have to play the devoted lover quite so assiduously?

With a faintly impatient movement, Margaret pulled the last page out of her machine and reached for the cover of her typewriter. As she did so, Giles leaned forward and put a small box on the desk beside her.

"That's for you," he said.

"For me?" She looked surprised. "Why? What is it?"

"Open it and see, if you can't guess." He looked amused, but somehow slightly vexed too.

She opened the box, found a small jewel case inside and exclaimed in a tone of something like dismay:

"It's a ring! Oh, Giles, do we have to do that? My goodness, what a beauty! But you shouldn't—Oh, how lovely! But there's no need——"

"Certainly there is. I'm not getting engaged to a girl without giving her a ring." He spoke impatiently, though he was smiling now at her wide-eyed admiration. "Do you like it?"

"Of course I do! I don't think I've ever seen a lovelier one." And Margaret stared, fascinated, at the diamond and sapphire which winked up at her from a curious and unusually beautiful setting.

"Shall I put it on for you?"

Some superstitious instinct told her that it was more binding if you let a man actually put an engagement ring on your finger. But she could hardly deny him that right, when he had gone to such trouble and expense to please her. In any case, even as she hesitated, she felt her hand taken in his long, strong fingers, and a second later the cool circlet of his ring slid on to her left hand.

At this moment—which was, after all, the climax of his friendly efforts on her behalf—Margaret would have liked to say something warm and appreciative. But the scene made her desperately nervous, and all she managed to say—and rather reprovingly at that—was:

"Giles, you shouldn't have got anything so—so utterly magnificent. It's much too beautiful for pretence."

"Do you have to bring pretence into it, just at this moment?" he asked, again in that half amused, half vexed way.

"Yes, I think I do!" She felt a little like someone trying to keep a foothold on an unexpectedly difficult slope. "I don't want to sound ungracious—and I think the ring is simply wonderful, Giles. But there's nothing *real* about all this, and——"

"Are you so sure, Meg?"

"What do you mean, am I sure?" She passed the tip of her tongue over suddenly dry lips.

"Don't look so scared." He actually laughed, though he bit his lip. "And don't think I'm trying to stampede you into anything. But there *are* things which have started as pretence and ended as reality, you know."

"Not this!" she said, quickly and more coldly than she had intended. And then, moved almost equally by her hopes and her fears in connection with the new situation developing round Paul, she felt impelled to define her position even more clearly. She would have preferred to take time to choose her words, so that she might soften the harshness of decision with some expression of her genuine gratitude. But again both nervousness and a sense of crisis drove her on.

"Giles, please don't get any romantic ideas about me or this absurd engagement," she heard herself say almost brusquely. "I'm grateful to you for your help, and I'm very sorry that we have to get ourselves involved in all the—the trimmings of a real engagement. But let's not pretend there's anything the remotest bit genuine about it. I'm not engaged to you, I'm not the slightest bit in love with you. And, if you're absolutely honest with yourself, it's the same with you."

"Sure?" He raised one eyebrow in the way Penelope admired.

"Completely sure. You're just rather intrigued and amused by the situation. It's not really much more than an enjoyable masquerade. Is it, now? Admit it."

She looked at him anxiously, almost pleadingly. And he looked back at her, with that half smile and the quizzical glance. Then he shrugged very slightly and said:

"If you say it's that way, then of course it is."

"But you know it is, yourself, don't you?" Somehow she needed some sort of reassurance on that point.

"I'll think it over again," he promised her lightly, "and see if I can come to your conclusion. Meanwhile, I want to thank you for your timely support yesterday evening, over Mother and Maxine."

"Oh, that's all right." She had almost forgotten their co-operation in that delicate family matter. But she was pleased to recall it now. To have done something for him, instead of having it all the other way round, made her feel less ungracious about having rejected his overtures for a closer friendship. And, as they went out to the car together, she asked with genuine warmth:

"How are things going to work out in that direction, do you think?"

"Pretty well. Mother is over the shock of finding that I have always maintained reasonably close contact with Maxine. And, now that she's discovered a creditable explanation for her own long silence, she feels she can allow herself the indulgence of breaking it." He grinned indulgently, as they settled themselves in the car.

"That's one way of looking at it," agreed Margaret dryly.

"Well, as I said before, when one's taken up an attitude that has hardened with the years, it's often necessary for someone else to indicate the way back."

"She's a very lucky woman to have such good children as you and Maxine," Margaret burst out. "I don't know who else would take so much trouble over saving her pride and indulging her foibles."

"If one can't take trouble over one's mother, for whom

should one bestir oneself?" he countered good-humouredly.

And, as that made Margaret a trifle ashamed of herself —and the undoubted dislike of Eileen which must have shown in her voice—she fell silent, and examined her ring, and found it even more beautiful than she had at first supposed.

If he noticed she was examining it afresh, he showed no interest in the fact. Instead, he concentrated on threading a way through the traffic, which was unexpectedly congested at this point.

"What's holding us up, do you suppose?" He leaned to one side and tried to see further ahead. "It's not a race meeting or anything, is it?"

"Not as far as I know." Rather guiltily, she withdrew her attention from her ring. And at that moment, there was the sound of an ambulance bell, away in front of them.

"There must have been an accident," they said with one voice and, at the same time, the stream of traffic began to move forward.

Even then, their progress was slow, and as they neared the crossroads and were stopped again, Giles leaned out of the side window to ask a lorry-driver coming in the opposite direction what had happened.

"Collision," he replied briefly. "Girl on her own in a red car. Women drivers!" And he cast up his eyes, as though calling on heaven to confirm his own low opinion of women drivers.

"Perhaps some careless man driver ran into her," said Margaret, promptly taking up the cudgels on behalf of her own sex. "They often do."

And then, quite suddenly, the description "girl on her own in a red car" took on an illogical and frightening significance. There were plenty of girls driving red cars, of course. And yet—She leaned across Giles and asked sharply:

"Who was it? Does anyone know?"

The lorry-driver shook his head and moved a few inches further on. But the driver of a private car coming on behind was evidently a local man, for he leaned out of his window, in his turn, and said:

"It was Percy Graham's girl, I'm afraid. You know—they have that nice place on the left-hand side, up towards Corbridge. She wasn't killed, but she looked pretty dicky when they rushed her off in the ambulance."

CHAPTER VII

"Giles!" Margaret exclaimed in horror. "It's Hester who has been hurt. Hester Graham. We must get home quickly. John will be frantic."

"John?" repeated Giles, with an upward jerk of his eyebrows, though he managed to ease the car forward a little more quickly, at the urgency in her tone. "Don't you mean Paul?"

"Oh——" She bit her lip at the slip. But then she decided that this crisis was going to bring a lot of things into the open, and she said, with a sort of desperate candour, "Paul too, of course. But I'm afraid the fact is that my poor John is also devoted to her."

"You don't say!" Giles looked sympathetic, though most of his attention was on his driving for, having at last got past the hold-up, he was letting out. "Did she turn John down before she took Paul, then? Somehow I didn't realize that the two families knew each other so well."

"They don't," Margaret told him. "And it's all rather —rather secret, Giles. She didn't turn John down first. It was *after* her engagement that he met her and fell for her."

"But how could it be?" Giles looked understandably astonished. "The engagement is only a day or two old."

"I know," Margaret said unhappily. "But he has only just met her. She came to the nurseries to buy flowers and it—happened. I know it sounds absurd and improbable, but I suppose these things do happen sometimes."

"Undoubtedly," he agreed, so seriously that she thought he must be laughing at her. But, when she glanced at him suspiciously, she saw that he had spoken with sincerity.

"Don't say anything about it to John, will you?" She was already regretting her confidence and felt she simply could not—indeed, should not—add the extraordinary fact that John obstinately believed that his love was returned.

"Of course not," Giles promised. "Perhaps the best thing is simply for me to assume that he is a friend of hers, and if he would like me to drive him down to the hospital, I will with pleasure."

"I think that might be a good attitude to take," Margaret agreed. Then she added, impulsively, "You're very kind, Giles, and you always seem to be doing nice, tactful things for this family when we're in trouble."

He laughed a disclaimer of that. But he flushed slightly too, at this unexpected tribute, and she saw that he was both pleased and touched.

When they arrived home, everything looked so normal and undisturbed that it was obvious no news of the accident had yet come in, even by way of the Emms grapevine. So Margaret went immediately in search of her brother.

She found him in the room that was sometimes called the study and sometimes the office—according to who was using it. He was poring over his accounts and, for a moment, she stood in the doorway, reluctant to wipe from his face the look of quiet contentment. But she could not delay.

"John——"

He looked up and said an absent, "Hello." But then he added, almost immediately, "My word, that's a beauty, and no mistake!"

"What is?" She was completely puzzled.

"What you've come to show me, I suppose." He laughed and gestured towards her left hand, which was grasping the edge of the door rather tightly. "Giles has done you proud, Meg, I must say."

"Oh—yes. Yes, hasn't he?" She glanced at her ring, if not with indifference, at least with a marked lack of the right kind of interest. "It's lovely, of course. But—John, I'm terribly sorry—I've really come about something else, and it isn't good news at all. Hester has had an accident——"

"Hester!" He was on his feet at once, pale and tense. "What sort of accident?"

"A car accident. It may not be terribly serious—I just don't know. Giles and I heard about it as we drove home. They've taken her to hospital, I imagine the local hospital rather than into Newcastle. And——"

"I must go to her." John spoke as though she were his concern only. "Has Father got the car?"

"I think he must have. It's not in the garage. But Giles says he will drive you down willingly."

"Giles? What does he know about it?"

"Well, he was with me, you see, when we heard. And I couldn't hide that I was upset, and as I had to tell him something, I told him that you and Hester were good friends. He isn't one to ask silly questions, John. In fact, he's marvellous in a crisis," she burst out earnestly, from the depths of personal experience. "He's waiting in the car now, out at the front of the house. You go. It's the quickest and best way."

John evidently thought so too. For, with the briefest word of thanks, he brushed past her and out of the room. And two minutes later she heard the car driving away from the house.

For a few seconds longer Margaret stood there, trying to think how she would explain the absence of the two men, and the excessive interest which they would appear to be taking in a mere acquaintance's affairs. But, finally deciding that she would have to speak according to the inspiration of the moment, she went out of the room— and immediately ran into an inquisitive Penelope.

"Where's John gone dashing off to?" she wanted to know. "He nearly knocked me over as he went tearing through the hall, and now he and Giles have gone off as though the police were after them."

"Well, they're not," replied Margaret, rather crossly, because she still had not thought of anything.

"I should've thought——" began Penelope. But then she caught sight of the new ring on her sister's finger and, with a squeal of rapture, she abandoned the subject of John and cried, "My goodness, what a beauty! It must have cost *heaps*. Do you think it cost as much as a hundred pounds?"

"I've no idea," Margaret said with truth. "You don't ask your fiancé what your ring costs, you know."

"Don't you?" Penelope seemed disappointed at what she obviously considered to be a mistaken sense of delicacy. "But it would be nice to know, wouldn't it? Do you think *I* could ask him?"

"No," said Margaret, simply and finally.

"Well, I shall tell Dorothy that I think it cost more than a hundred pounds," declared Penelope, determined not to be done out of her little moment of pride. "I'm sure it did, and I'm sure he loves you at least as much as a hundred pounds."

"I hope so." Margaret smiled slightly, whereupon Penelope became embarrassingly romantic and asked point blank:

"Did Giles put it on your finger himself and kiss you?"

Somehow, this artless query brought back with great clarity the odd moment when Giles had put the ring on her finger. And, although he had not in point of fact kissed her, Margaret found herself colouring slightly as she said, "Yes."

"Everything's terribly exciting, isn't it?" Penelope sucked in her cheeks, thoughtfully and with relish. "Things simply keep on happening. First Father getting married—though of course that wasn't very exciting for *us*—and then your getting engaged, and then my finding that I'm really an aunt. I wonder whatever is going to happen next."

Margaret wondered too. But, refraining from making forecasts, she went instead to her own room to get ready for dinner.

Since the absence of Giles and John would certainly

have to be explained then, she took the initiative as soon as the others had assembled and said:

"It's no good our waiting for Giles and John. They've both gone to the hospital to make inquiries about Hester Graham. I'm afraid she had a car accident——"

"Hester Graham?" exclaimed Eileen and her husband in concert, and Mr. Masters added, "I'm very sorry to hear that. How did it happen?"

Margaret explained what little she knew of the accident, and then Eileen said:

"But why did *they* go to make inquiries? They hardly know her, surely?"

"John knows her—and her parents," Margaret said coolly, "and Giles kindly drove him there, as Father had our car out."

"I didn't know John knew the Grahams." Mr. Masters looked surprised. "No one mentioned it on——"

"It's quite recent, Father," Margaret interrupted quickly. "I think Hester has been in sometimes for flowers, and last week she left her compact or something. John took it back to her on Sunday—yesterday, I mean," she added, a good deal surprised herself to find that it was all so recent. "He said both the Grahams were particularly kind, and kept him to tea. I suppose he felt the least he could do was to go and make kind inquiries, now that the daughter has had this unfortunate accident."

"Of course, of course," Mr. Masters agreed, quite satisfied with the explanation. But Eileen, characteristically, had other views to express.

"I sometimes think it's a little kinder to hold back at these times, instead of rushing in with panic-stricken inquiries," she said, with the pensive air of one who always considered the feelings of others first. "I'm sure they meant well. But I should have thought a telephone call to the hospital would have been sufficient—and more considerate."

"Possibly they felt the hospital exchange shouldn't be overloaded with casual inquiries," replied Margaret dryly. "One wouldn't want to block the line for urgent calls. Her own family might be trying to get through, for all they knew."

"Perhaps I'm a little over-sensitive about these things," Eileen's hostile glance belied the thought. "But I always think——"

"Anyway," interrupted her husband brusquely, "if John can be of any use, he should certainly be there and willing to act in a neighbourly way. I'm very sorry about it. They seemed such a nice, devoted family. And of course, the girl had only just got engaged, hadn't she? What about him? Was he driving?"

"No. She was alone in the car, according to a passer-by. And as for Paul Freemantle——" Margaret got the name out with admirable coolness—"I think he's abroad on some assignment for his paper."

"I bet he'll come rushing home, though," observed Penelope, evidently seeing the whole thing in the satisfying and dramatic terms of the cinema, with the returning hero leaping in and out of planes and cars.

"He may not be able to," said Margaret. And suddenly her heart ached for Paul, far away in a foreign country, perhaps unable to get home, even though he knew the girl he loved was dangerously ill, and it seemed to her in that moment that her brother—dearly though she loved him—had a very unfair advantage.

"But he'll make himself free," declared Eileen. "Of course he will! Any man worth his salt would do so."

Then, before Margaret could argue, on Paul's behalf, about the impossibility sometimes of putting private affairs before professional ones, Penelope exclaimed:

"Here they are, back again. There's the car."

It was the car indeed. But it was only Giles who came into the room a moment later.

"Well, how is she?" inquired everyone in chorus.

"Not too good, I'm afraid." Giles looked grave. "She has pretty serious head injuries. I've left John there."

"Left John there?" It was his mother who took it upon

herself to query that. "Isn't that rather—pushing of him?
After all, he's only——"

"No, Mother. It was very nice and helpful of him,"
replied Giles dryly. "Both Hester's parents are quite
distracted, and seemed uncommonly glad to have John's
support. He's a very calm and reassuring sort of person,
and I can quite imagine that he's a comfort to them."

"Very gratifying to hear that," observed Mr. Masters,
ignoring his wife's faintly petulant expression. "How
long is he likely to be there?"

"I've promised to go back in an hour for him," Giles
explained. "And I thought perhaps Margaret——" he
looked inquiringly in her direction—"might come with
me. Mrs. Graham is a good deal distressed and——"

"Perhaps it would be better if *I* came, dear." Eileen
was annoyed at being left out of this. "After all, an older
woman——"

"No, Mother." Giles was unexpectedly quite equal to
this. "It's not the place for anyone who's sensitive and
easily upset."

Eileen started to say that she always exercised great
self-control in an emergency. But Giles merely turned to
Mr. Masters and said :

"I hope you'll exercise your authority, sir, and per-
suade Mother to leave this to Margaret and me. She tends
to take on too much, and——"

"I quite agree!" Mr. Masters immediately assumed
the rather heavily protective air which Eileen, as "the
little woman", usually enjoyed, but which on this
occasion obviously caused her some irritation. "Giles and
Margaret can manage perfectly well, you know. And,
after all, they expect to do things together now."

Margaret dared not look at her stepmother, to see how
she took the tactless underlining of this unpalatable
truth. She just said quietly to Giles, "I'll be ready when
you are."

And later they drove down to the hospital, without
further hindrance.

It was a neat, pleasant cottage hospital, with an atmosphere that was both homely and efficient. A very pretty, quiet-voiced nurse explained that a specialist had been summoned from Newcastle and that he was, even now, operating. And then she took them to a bright, cheerful-looking waiting-room, where they found poor Mrs. Graham, stirring a cup of tea in unhappy concentration, without ever attempting to drink it.

On hearing that John and Mr. Graham were strolling up and down in the grounds at the back of the hospital, Giles took himself off to join them, and Margaret stayed to keep Mrs. Graham company.

"It was so kind of you to come, dear." Mrs. Graham, who had obviously once been nearly as pretty and lively as her daughter, wiped away a couple of tears and gazed at Margaret gratefully from singularly innocent blue eyes. "But then you really are a most kind family. I don't know what my husband and I would have done without your brother. We've only met him once, and yet he just appeared—from nowhere, as you might say—almost as soon as we got here. And he's been such a comfort ever since."

"I'm sure he would be only too glad to help." Margaret poured out a fresh cup of tea and persuaded Mrs. Graham to drink it. "I know myself how quiet and comforting John can be."

"Yes, indeed!" A little colour had come back into the older woman's cheeks, now that she had drunk the tea. "He was simply wonderful with my husband. You know what fathers are over their daughters. And Hester is our only one, of course, and such a d—darling."

"Everyone says what a dear girl she is," Margaret agreed earnestly. "I can't tell you how much we all feel with you and Mr. Graham. But do try to be hopeful, dear Mrs. Graham, and don't distress yourself too much. I believe the man they've brought from Newcastle is absolutely marvellous, and I feel sure they're going to bring us some good news soon."

She was not sure at all, of course. But—like all of us in similar circumstances—she had to fall back on optimistic generalities in order to keep the more specific fears at bay. In Mrs. Graham's case, this seemed to work as well as anything else, for she dried her eyes, and even smiled very faintly at Margaret, as she said:

"I'll try. I think it's a little easier for women, don't you? We're used to keeping up our hearts. Men seem to feel so helpless when anything like this happens. Percy—that's my husband, you know—was quite frantic. But your brother seemed to know just what to say to him. Not silly things, but really sensible and reassuring words."

Margaret was both touched and surprised to hear this. Because, though she had never doubted John's goodness of heart, she had also never thought of him as specially good at managing people. But, with the Grahams, it seemed that he knew how to speak their language—just as though there were some subtle bond between him and even Hester's parents.

"He spoke so *kindly*." Poor Mrs. Graham, who had been overlong alone, appeared now unable to stem the tide of her own eloquence, and Margaret did not try to stop her, knowing very well that, while she was talking of John's excellence, she could, by the smallest fraction, keep herself removed from her fears for Hester.

"He used words that really warmed my heart," Mrs. Graham declared. "He said so simply, 'I know what you're feeling, Mrs. Graham. I love her too. No one who knew her could help loving her.' Wasn't that wonderful of him?—so simply and warmly said—'I love her too, Mrs. Graham.' I just don't know another young man who would speak with that kind frankness."

"I'm very glad if he found the right words," Margaret said, and, glancing at Mrs. Graham's pale, slightly tear-stained face, she saw that for the older woman there had been no particular significance about John's choice of words. She simply thought that he was speaking of her beloved Hester in the kindest terms he could—and, in return, she loved him for it.

Margaret was not quite sure if it were anxious curiosity which prompted her next words or an obscure feeling that *someone* must speak up for the absent Paul, even if it had to be herself. But she heard herself say:

"Have you sent for—for Hester's fiancé, Mrs. Graham?"

"Paul?" Mrs. Graham looked faintly startled. "Oh, poor boy, of course—he'll have to know. But I don't know where we can find him. He's abroad. Hester would know his address, of course, but we can't ask her, poor child."

"His paper would know where to find him," Margaret pointed out.

"Yes—yes, of course. As soon as we know—when they tell us, I mean——"

Poor Mrs. Graham's voice trailed away, as they heard quick light steps in the corridor outside.

"Oh, dear——" whispered the older woman, as though she desperately feared the next few minutes. And, guessing how she felt, Margaret took her hand in a firm, warm clasp, as a middle-aged Sister, with a brisk manner but very kindly eyes, came into the room.

"All right, Mrs. Graham," she said, with blessed lack of delay. "The news is pretty good. Mr. Linform thinks the emergency operation is successful, though she isn't out of the wood yet. It was most fortunate that we were able to get hold of him so quickly. Time was everything."

"Then you mean—she'll be all right? *Quite* all right?" Mrs. Graham's tears were flowing openly, in the anguish of relief.

"It's too early to make absolutely confident statements," the Sister said kindly. "But Mr. Linform is very satisfied. She's a lovely, healthy girl, as I don't need to tell you—and we're going to take the utmost care of her. I think we'll have her completely well in time, Mrs. Graham."

"Oh, how wonderful! I'm so grateful! The relief is

almost too much. I must tell my husband—where is he?"

"Mr. Linform is with him and your son now."

"My son?" Mrs. Graham looked puzzled. "I haven't got a son."

"I'm sorry! I thought the young man with you——"

"Oh, no—no, that's a young friend of ours. But he seems just like a son," Mrs. Graham burst out. "He couldn't have been kinder if he had been." And, overcome by her relief and her gratitude to John, she buried her face in her handkerchief and wept.

Margaret and the Sister exchanged a sympathetic glance. Then Margaret put her arms round the older woman and hugged her comfortingly, though the unforced tribute to her brother had brought something of a lump into her own throat.

"Hester's going to be all right now, remember," she said. "You can have a few tears of relief, but then you must really cheer up and smile, or your husband will think the news isn't so good, after all."

"Yes, yes—of course. I must stop being such a fool," Mrs. Graham agreed, with a watery smile. "And if Percy and John would come now——"

Percy and John were presently found and, since neither of the older Grahams seemed to think that a family discussion would be complete without John, Margaret left them together and went to join Giles.

It was a fine, warm evening, and this time it was they who walked up and down in the hospital grounds, until John should be free to go home with them.

"Nice couple," commented Giles. "I'm glad their girl is going to be all right. She's evidently their whole world."

"Yes. I'm glad too we were able to keep them company during these bad hours. At least—John seems to have been a great help."

"Yes. It's odd how he seems to fit into the picture, as though they had known each other always. What's the real situation, Meg?"

"I hardly know, myself," Margaret confessed, "and I too can't quite understand how it is that the Grahams seem to accept John and rely on him, as though he were one of the family. One would almost think——"

She stopped, but Giles completed the sentence for her, quite calmly.

"You'd think he was the fiancé, wouldn't you?" he said.

Margaret made a little gesture with her hands that was half protest, half agreement.

"What is Hester's reaction to all this, do you know?"

"I only know John is convinced that she has some feeling for him too. I've never seen them together, Giles. To tell the truth, I've never exchanged a word with her; only seen her occasionally, at dances or in the street. So it isn't possible to judge even how she *might* react to all this. No one can dispute the fact that she's engaged to Paul—and yet John considers himself madly in love with her, and is sure she recognizes him as the real man in her life."

"Which would make our little masquerade rather unnecessary, wouldn't it—or would it?"

"What do you mean?" She glanced at him quickly.

"If the Paul-Hester engagement falls through——". He did not complete the sentence, and for nearly a minute they paced the paths of the hospital garden in silence. Then, as she would have turned towards the building again, he took her firmly by the arm and walked her on, until the trees and shrubs at the end of the garden hid them from any possible observation from the hospital windows.

"Giles, what is it?" She saw that his expression was unusually determined and unsmiling.

"I've got to talk to you, Meg. Not just on the surface of things, as we've been doing continually. I've got to talk about the essential *us*."

"Oh, does it have to be now?" The protest was half apprehensive.

"Yes, it does," he said curtly. And, although the hand

round her arm held her lightly, she had the impression
that it would have been difficult to get away.

"Well?" She had not meant that to sound cold, but,
even in her own ears, it was hardly encouraging.

"Meg, I didn't think things could get much more
tangled—but they have. If Hester breaks her engagement and takes John instead——"

"Isn't that absurdly improbable?" countered Margaret, against all her inmost conviction and hope.

"The absurdly improbable sometimes happens," Giles
replied dryly. "One has to take it into consideration. And
I want to know—*if* that happened, are you cherishing the
idea that Paul would come back to you?"

"Please——" she winced angrily at the almost brutal
candour of that—"can't you mind your own business—
at least about faint possibilities that may never happen?"

"No," he said, without qualification. "Even faint
possibilities have an alarming appearance when one's
deepest interests are involved."

"What do you mean by that, exactly?"

"What you're trying so desperately to prevent me from
saying," he retorted. "Meg——" suddenly he took hold
of her by both her arms and turned her to face him completely—"Meg, I love you. This pretended engagement
is not a pretence to me. I was glad when circumstances
thrust it upon us, because I wanted it. I was happy to be
the one to whom you turned. When I saw that fool who'd
hurt and insulted you finally turn his back, it was all I
could do not to help him off the scene with a final
kick."

"Don't be ridiculous!" Nervousness and indignation
sharpened her tone. "How dare you talk of Paul like
that? He's worth——" She stopped suddenly, aware that
she had been about to make an absurd claim on Paul's
behalf.

But Giles caught her up on that half-uttered protest.

"Well?" he said almost challengingly. "What is he
worth? Ten of me, were you going to say? That isn't

true, you know. He may have charm and he may have swept you off your feet once. But he's lightweight, Meg, and totally unreliable. Put him out of your mind, whether Hester takes him or not. He's not *worth* your thought and your affection. Don't you know that?"

"I won't discuss it!" She spoke breathlessly. "I'm not giving any undertaking to *you*. If Paul were free again——"

Once more she stopped abruptly. And, after a moment, he said softly:

"Well—if Paul were free again?—That's what I'm trying to ask you."

"I can't tell you," she cried. "I can't discuss the position in theory."

"It's not in theory. It's completely practical. I'm asking you to put Paul out of your mind, once and for all. I'm asking you to marry me, Meg. Really marry me. To turn this fake engagement into a genuine one. Not to wait and see if he'll graciously come back to you, once he's free. I love you, and——"

"No, no, no!" she cried, with such emphasis that he was instantly silenced. "I love Paul. Whether he's free or tied, whether he wants me or not, I love Paul. I'm only wearing your ring now because I have to. I'm only listening to you now because the world expects us to share each other's company. But there's nothing real about it. I'm grateful for what you did——"

"I don't want gratitude," he interrupted violently.

"It's all I have to give you," she replied, nearly as violently. And, for a moment, they looked into each other's eyes almost like enemies. Then he said, much more softly:

"Are you sure, my darling? Are you quite, quite sure that you're not clinging to an old illusion, and rejecting something that *is* real? You did turn to me, you know, when he wanted you to kiss him that last time. You turned from him—and to me."

"But that was just instinctive," she protested. "I

dared not let him kiss me, even lightly, for fear he guessed how I really felt. I had to turn to you. There was no one else," she added, with devastating simplicity.

"I see."

His hands dropped from her arms, and she was suddenly free to go. But, illogically, that was the moment when she wanted to stay and explain herself—urgently, eagerly and (however much he might hate the word) gratefully.

"I'm sorry, Giles." She clasped and unclasped her hands nervously. "I'm truly sorry. I don't want to hurt you, when you've been so good to me. But one can't love, or not love, by rule of argument."

"That's true." He sounded cool and agreeable, almost academic as though the matter no longer concerned him.

"You're angry with me now, but I can't help——"

"I'm not at all angry with you. I'm rather angry with myself for forcing this on you at the wrong time. But I'm not angry with you, Meg. One can't love to order, or by argument, as you said. I wish I could tell you to forget this conversation, but it would be absurd to pretend that either of us could. Only—don't let it make you feel even worse than you do about our pretended engagement, will you?"

"I'll try not to."

"I'm willing to see you through this engagement, to whatever point you choose." He spoke as though it were a business deal, in which he was prepared to play a fair part, but no more. "And don't make yourself uneasy over anything we have to do or say in order to make our position seem more plausible. I've accepted quite finally now that the whole thing is pretence, and pretence only. Does that make you feel a bit better about things?"

She said that it did, because the idea of trying to clarify their impossible situation any further was something she simply could not face. But in actual fact she felt dreadful. Not that she in any way mistrusted his undertaking to keep things strictly on the level of pretence in future.

But because his easy generosity made her feel that she herself was being mean.

Besides, by the simplest rules of decency, when a girl refused a man's proposal, at least she showed some sort of appreciation of having been asked. But she, on the contrary, she realized, had made it crystal clear that she found his offer an embarrassment and a burden. At no point had she found either the grace or the good feeling to thank him at least for loving her.

It was not really in Margaret to reject any friendly or affectionate approach without regret. And, at the realization of her ungenerosity, she actually felt the tears sting her eyes. But the time for nice speeches was long past. The situation had come upon her unawares, and she had dealt with it on the spur of the moment, as well—or, she feared, as badly—as she could. Few declarations of love could have been received less gracefully. But there was nothing she could do about it now.

As they turned their steps towards the hospital building once more, she glanced anxiously at him. There was no resentment in his strong, good-looking face, as far as she could see. Only an extreme thoughtfulness.

The agitating scene must have left far more traces on *her* face, she felt. In fact, even now, she shrank inwardly at the thought of the spate of words and argument which had poured over them. Some of it had become only a confused and painful jumble now. But some things stuck there in her memory, burning their way into her consciousness.

And, to her dismay and anger, the words which came back to her most persistently and with inescapable clarity were the words he had used about Paul.

"He's lightweight, Meg, and totally unreliable. He's not *worth* your thought and your affection."

CHAPTER VIII

For some days the Grahams, and all who wished them well, were kept in a state of considerable anxiety. Hester made good headway at first, but then there was a slight relapse. And it was during this period that Paul came home at last.

The report of his arrival came, incongruously enough, from John, who was at the hospital every day, for quite long periods. But he added nothing to the simple statement of fact.

Eileen said rather censoriously to Margaret that she thought John was making himself just a little bit conspicuous.

"Why should *he* identify himself so much with the Grahams?" she wanted to know. "He seems consumed with curiosity about that poor girl. I should have thought he could have left the inquiries and the good wishes to your father and to me. After all, the Grahams are *our* friends."

"No more than they are John's friends," replied Margaret, with admirable self-control. Because the last thing she wanted to have was an acrimonious dispute on the subject with Eileen—and perhaps some shrewd guesswork. "I think the fact is that the Grahams found him very useful and sympathetic when the accident first happened, and they quite naturally look to him to help them in keeping up their spirits. Besides, they're tied at the hospital for most of the day, and no doubt he can do lots of odd jobs for them. I don't know why you should hold it against him that he's kind and neighbourly, Eileen."

"I don't hold it against him, dear," said her stepmother, who could say "dear" more offensively than anyone else Margaret had ever come across. "You mustn't put words into my mouth like that. I only feel that it's rather insensitive and *immature* to try to gather personal importance from the misfortunes of someone else, don't you?"

Margaret bit her lip until it actually hurt. But she then managed to keep her tone quite mild as she replied:

"I don't think Mr. and Mrs. Graham regard John's behaviour at all as you do. And, after all, they are the people to be considered at the moment, aren't they?"

"Well, I don't know. Now that Paul Freemantle has come home, I suppose even John will accept the fact that he isn't needed." And Eileen smiled with infuriating sweetness, while Margaret felt her heart both heavy and elated by those words.

For if Paul had come home to take his rightful position with Hester, then her brother, whom she loved dearly, faced crushing disappointment and unhappiness. On the other hand, if Paul had come home to find himself largely supplanted—what then?

Her own affairs had gone surprisingly smoothly after that agitating scene with Giles in the hospital garden. Her family were, in some way, used to the engagement now, and took it for granted that they should spend a good deal of time together, without—except in Penelope's case—seeming to think that demonstrations of open affection were called for.

Penelope, however, was not entirely satisfied.

"You'd think you were *married*, the way you take each other for granted," she said to Margaret, with innocent cynicism. "You never sort of sit in corners and hold each other's hands."

"It doesn't take us that way," replied Margaret calmly.

"Well, Dorothy says that when her cousin Bertha was engaged she and her Ronald were simply *sickening*," Penelope told her reprovingly.

"Do you want Giles and me to be sickening?"

"No, not as bad as that. But you *are* really in love with each other, aren't you?" demanded Penelope categorically.

"Of course," said Margaret, feeling base in the extreme, for there was something touching as well as absurd about her little sister's anxiety to find that all the values were correct.

"Well, I'm glad of that. Because I think Giles is the kind one *should* love," was Penelope's unexpected verdict. "He's too nice not to be loved."

It was a statement so staggering in its simplicity and basic truth that Margaret felt absurdly shaken.

Pen was right, of course. Giles *was* too nice not to be loved. He deserved the best. And, although she was certainly not guilty of wishing a loveless marriage on to him, she had undoubtedly wished a painful and equivocal engagement on to him. It was, she supposed uneasily, hard to imagine anything worse than to love someone and have to go through the motions of being engaged, while knowing all the time that it was as empty and savourless as an Indiarubber ball.

Her little sister's words disturbed her so much that, in that moment, Margaret was sorely tempted to break off the so-called engagement then and there, and take whatever consequences there might be. But, almost instantly, she knew this was impossible. Quite apart from the bewilderment and awkwardness there would be in the family circle, she *had* to know about Paul first. She simply could not have his suspicions aroused afresh by a strangely shortened engagement.

So she murmured some general agreement to Penelope's expressed views, and hoped that she would have no more difficulty in that direction.

Not that Penelope was by any means the most difficult person where her engagement was concerned. Eileen too displayed the most unwelcome curiosity, and hers was of a jealous bitterness.

"You take it all so coolly, Margaret," she said once. "I sometimes wonder if you know what a lucky girl you are."

"I think and hope I do." Margaret spoke as pacifically as she could. "To me Giles is one in a million."

That at least was true. Because she could not imagine that more than one man in a million would have come to her aid in the way Giles had.

"Oh, you do know that, do you?" Eileen regarded her without favour. "I thought perhaps you had the idea that *he* was lucky to get *you*."

"I don't think either of us regards the other in that light, Eileen," said Margaret, wondering uneasily if that sounded as stilted and pompous to her stepmother as it did to herself. But it was so terribly difficult to speak in anything but the most general terms when the particular case was so delicate.

"You're so cold, somehow." Eileen looked reproachful about the eyes and hard about the mouth. "I know I'm perhaps almost too impulsive and sensitive. But I should have thought you could show a little more feeling."

"I don't wear my heart on my sleeve," replied Margaret, still leaning heavily on platitudes.

"No. You're extraordinarily secretive for a girl," agreed her stepmother sharply. "And I must tell you, dear, that it isn't very attractive. I had hoped that, as his *mother*, I should have been treated with a little more warmth and—oh, I don't know—more confidingly. You've never once asked me loving questions about him. And there's so much I could tell you which only a mother knows. Isn't there *anything* that you want to ask me about him, Margaret?"

There was not. And for an uncomfortable instant Margaret's mind went quite blank. Then, with a great effort, she managed to say, almost pleasantly:

"I expect we see him from different angles, Eileen. I'm not being deliberately secretive, I assure you. But I—I don't think I can discuss Giles with you—or anyone else."

"Funny child!" Eileen gave a deprecating little laugh. Then she sighed and said, "I suppose I'm just so different that I can't understand. Your father says I feel almost *too* deeply about the people I love."

Margaret could think of no brilliant comment to make

on this odd conclusion of her father's, so she remained silent, until Eileen—very brave and wistful—said:

"I try not to feel hurt about losing Giles. Though, of course, I know I should never really lose him—to any-one," she added quickly. "But for years he was all I had, and I expect that's partly why he has such a very, very special place in my heart."

"Well, now you have Father, haven't you?" For the life of her, Margaret could not help speaking a trifle bracingly. "And Maxine—and the children. When are you going to see them, Eileen?"

Eileen said, a little repressively, that one had to con-dition oneself to the thought of such an emotional re-union. And there they left things.

Unexpectedly, it was to Margaret that Maxine tele-phoned that very same evening, with the information that she would be in Newcastle for the afternoon later that week, and was there any chance of Margaret meeting her there.

"I don't want our first meeting to be an isolated occasion," she said, the full tones of her gay, warm voice coming clearly over the wire. "Besides, it's ages since I had anyone with whom I could have a girlish gossip, and I'd love it if we could get together. What do you say, Margaret?"

Margaret said, quite truthfully, that she would like nothing better, but that she would have to ask her father if she could have the afternoon off, and would telephone back later.

Then she sought out her father at a moment when Eileen was otherwise employed, and put the proposition to him.

He agreed with unexpected alacrity.

"Yes, that's right. You go and see her, Meg, and try to soften up that hard attitude of hers towards Eileen," he said warmly. "Heaven knows how a girl could be like that to any mother—least of all Eileen. Take the full day, my dear. There are one or two things I want in Newcastle, and I can't very well bother Eileen to get them. Besides, you know what I like. I'll give you a list, and you can see to everything."

Mr. Masters was very cheerful at the thought of having his personal commissions attended to once more by his capable daughter. And Margaret, on her side, looked forward with real pleasure to a free day in town. For, though she genuinely liked her office life, like everyone who has once known freedom, she was sometimes a good deal irked by the necessary routine and restrictions.

She told Giles about the proposed meeting, and he seemed to understand immediately that, on this occasion, his sister and she preferred to be on their own. And, though Margaret laid no special prohibition on him, she gathered that he did not mention the matter to Eileen, for there was no comment from that quarter, which there certainly would have been if her stepmother had thought Margaret was, as she would have put it, interfering again.

It was an enchanting day when Margaret set out for Newcastle. One of those cool, shimmering days of early summer, when there is a pearly quality to the light, which one sees only in the northern counties.

She miscalculated her bus times slightly and, on finding that she had a quarter of an hour to wait, she crossed the road to the nurseries, and went in to have a word with John. She had hardly seen him during the last two days, for he had left the house early and returned very late, either because he was catching up on work neglected during Hester's illness, or because he still spent all of his spare time at the hospital; Margaret was not sure which.

He was standing at a high desk, making entries in a ledger, when she came into the little office, and she thought, with a sudden pang, that he was thinner than she had ever seen him, and that some deep emotion—anxiety, she supposed—had carved lines on his young face which had never been there before.

He smiled, however, as he looked up to greet her. And,

when she explained that she had a quarter of an hour to wait for her bus, he pushed forward a chair for her.

"Any fresh news of Hester this morning?" she inquired, as she sat down.

"I phoned the hospital, and she's picking up well again. She's made up all the ground she lost during that relapse."

It occurred to Margaret that Paul's return might have had something to do with this. But she only said:

"How long before they think she can go home, John?"

"Oh, no one's even mentioned that yet." He shook his head. "She's still very weak, you know. Hardly even speaks much. Though she smiled and said a few words to me yesterday."

"You still see her every day?"

"Of course." He looked so astonished at the idea of his doing anything else that she felt bound to explain:

"I thought perhaps—after Paul came home——"

"Oh, that." He smiled. "We haven't run into each other."

"That's a good thing," said Margaret. Then she thought what a perfectly idiotic thing that was to say, in the circumstances; and finally how impossible it was, really, to discuss this thing with her brother or anyone else while no one knew how Hester was going to react when she returned to the world she had so very nearly left.

There seemed nothing more for either of them to say, and Margaret was silent until she heard her bus coming. Then she bade her brother goodbye, and went out into the sunshine again, feeling disturbed and frustrated and curiously helpless.

The feeling passed, once she was on her way. And, putting all problems aside, she prepared to enjoy a busy morning's shopping, and then a pleasant, relaxed afternoon with Maxine.

It was one of those rare mornings when everything went well. Nothing was out of stock, everything was easily available, so that her commissions were attended to much sooner than she expected. She came out of Fenwicks, the last purchase made, and paused for a moment in the sunshine, to savour the pleasant fact that she was free in the middle of the day, with no one to consult but herself.

She had almost forgotten the delicious feeling of being on holiday while all the world was working and she was smiling her appreciation of it when someone came up beside and said:

"I gather the world is a very good place at the moment."

"Paul!"

She turned to him with a flashing glance of such open joy that he gave a pleased little laugh and took her by the arm.

"Well, I'm delighted to find *someone* who's glad to see me home," he observed, so lightly that she did not gather the real significance of that at the moment. "What about a spot of lunch? I've a table at Tilleys, and if you're free——"

"Oh, yes, I'm free." She tried to keep the lilt out of her voice, but failed. "That was really why I was standing there smiling, I think. I have the day off."

"From family chores?"

"Oh, no. From the office. I work in Father's office now, you know."

"I didn't know. I don't seem to know anything much about you these days, Meg. Except that you're engaged to Giles Ormby, lucky fellow!"

"Well, let's—let's go and have lunch, then, and exchange all our news," she exclaimed, with a gaiety that was lighthearted or lightheaded, she was not quite sure which. And she was keenly aware that his hand remained round her arm, his fingers pressing her lightly, as he guided her across the road and the short distance to their destination.

He had a secluded corner table, of course. Paul was the kind of man who was always looked after well in restaurants. And, when they were seated, he leaned his arms on the table, smiled full at her and said :

"You look lovely, Meg."

She had known she was looking quite nice, even before that. But when Paul said she was lovely, it was as though a lamp lit up inside her, and she smiled at him and saw, in the mirror opposite, that she was indeed lovely.

"Happiness must suit you," he told her.

"Doesn't it suit us all ?"

"I guess so. If it comes our way." He sighed quickly and, reaching for the menu, began to consult her about what she would like.

At that moment, she would willingly have settled for dry bread and water, if that had been his suggestion. But fortunately Paul was a man who appreciated good food and wine, and the meal he selected would have satisfied a much more sophisticated taste than Margaret's.

Then, that business settled, he smiled at her again and said, "Now tell me all the news."

"I think you must tell me yours first," she countered quickly. "How is Hester ?" For, though she felt a bit deceitful, it would never have done for her to let him know that she had all the latest news through John.

"Much better, I'm glad to say." But a faintly discontented, clouded look came over his face, perhaps at the recollection of past anxiety. "She's been terribly ill, Margaret."

"Yes, I know. Everyone was dreadfully upset. It caused quite a stir, because she's a very popular girl. Giles and I happened to be passing, just a few minutes after the accident, and I—I went to the hospital and was with Mrs. Graham while they waited for Mr. Linform to operate."

"I didn't know you knew them."

"I didn't—much. But Father and Eileen had visited them only a few days before. And John had met her several times." She thought she had got that out very naturally. But to her dismay, Paul fixed her with a thoughtful glance at that, and said bluntly :

"What's going on there, Meg?"

"H—How do you mean?" She was indescribably put out, and maintained her innocent glance only with the greatest difficulty.

"Your brother John has visited her every day since this happened, hasn't he? and he's the white-headed boy, so far as Hester's parents are concerned."

"Oh——" She glanced down and, without knowing it, nervously traced a pattern on the cloth with her finger. "I wouldn't know much about that, Paul. I see quite astonishingly little of John these days. He's out, working hard, from early morning to late at night, and as for me, I'm off to the Works——"

"He hasn't been working solidly from dawn to dusk all these days," Paul interrupted shortly. "He's been up and down to the hospital quite a lot of the time."

"How do you know that?" She managed to look up again then, though she had some difficulty in meeting his eyes.

"One of the nurses mentioned it, quite by chance, before she knew who I was. She was rather obstructive about my going in and said only the parents and Mr. Masters visited regularly. Then I tackled Mrs. Graham, and she was distinctly off-putting, saying something about John Masters having been like a son to them. And I may say that, from her tone, I wondered if she didn't mean 'like a son-in-law'," he finished, with an angry little laugh.

"I do know John made himself very—neighbourly and useful——" She wondered how many more times she was going to have to apply this innocuous phrase to a dangerous situation—"and I suppose they were glad to have his help. After all, they must have missed you and——"

"Nobody missed me, so far as I can make out," was the dry retort. "Not even Hester."

"Oh, Paul!" She was genuinely shocked. Partly by his candour, and partly because of his disturbingly quick summing up of the position. Then, after a moment and because she simply could not help it, she asked, almost fearfully, "Why do you say Hester didn't miss you? She's been so very ill that I suppose she must have been vague about time and perhaps not realized that you were missing for some days."

"Possibly. But there were other things that were vague as well as time. She was rather vague about whether or not she wanted to see me. And my visit was cut to a matter of minutes."

"But she's *ill*, Paul. She's still very ill. I can't think that they allow long visits to anyone."

"Not even your brother?" he said sardonically.

"I have no idea when or for how long he sees her." She was glad to be able to state at least that with the conviction of truth. "But I can well imagine that no one sees her for long."

"I wonder." He looked moodily at her across the table.

"Paul, don't you think you might be imagining things?" She longed to comfort him, and she hated to be disingenuous with him. But the secret she was guarding was not hers to give away.

"Yes," he agreed, "I *could* be imagining things, of course. But I don't think I am."

She was silent at that. And then, to her mingled relief and fresh alarm, he roused himself from his rather moody silence to say:

"Let's talk of something else, more cheerful. Let's talk of you, Meg."

Almost any subject was better than that of Hester and John. But over her own affairs she would have to tread almost as warily. She smiled at him, however, with what lightness she could muster and said:

"Well, as I told you, I'm working in Father's office now."

"So the family didn't need you all that desperately, Meg." He suddenly imprisoned her hand on the table with one of his, and his glance was half teasing, half reproachful. "Remember? They just had to be the first consideration, in the days when I was trying to make you listen to me."

"Th—things were different then," she protested, with slightly dry lips. "They had only me. And then, when Eileen came, quite frankly it was all rather impossible at home."

"Was it? Serves you right!" But he smiled at her so affectionately as he let her hand go that she found she was trembling.

A little desperately, Margaret decided that Eileen must be sacrificed to the necessity of giving the conversation a harmless turn. So she treated him to a lighthearted and amusing account of Eileen's impact upon the Masters household.

He laughed a good deal and was genuinely curious.

"You mean that Elinor actually left home because of her?"

"Not entirely. She was already flirting with the idea of a place of her own, I realize now. But the change at home was the deciding factor. She would never have got along with Eileen, Paul."

"And you? How do you get along with her?"

"I make myself do so. I'm just determined not to have open warfare, for the sake of Pen and Father."

"And Giles, I take it?"

"Well, of course."

"But she's going to be a formidable mother-in-law, isn't she?" The situation intrigued him, she saw.

"I'll work that one out when the time comes."

"And when *does* it come, Meg? What are the plans? Are you having quite a short engagement?"

"Oh, no, no," she said hastily. "We haven't fixed on any date yet. There's no hurry."

He gave her a quizzical glance.

"Is that his view too?" And when she didn't answer, he added, "Just the opposite from me, eh? I tried too hard to hurry you—and you always hung back."

"Paul, I *had* to. You don't suppose I wanted to. Why, I——"

She stopped, frightened by what she had been about to say. And at that he grinned reflectively at her and said:

"It's like old times, isn't it? Arguing with each other across a table at Tilleys."

Nostalgia hit her like a wave, and she gasped a little as she went under. Then she heard him say musingly:

"I wonder if one ever would act differently, if one could turn back the pages."

"But one never can turn them back, can one? So one never finds out," she replied, because she had to say something.

"Never, Meg?" He had her hand again now, and she held his tightly, as though she feared another wave and must hold on to something.

She waited, trembling with unspeakable eagerness for the next word. But when it came, the voice was an entirely different one, and it spoke above the level of her bent head.

"Hello, Meg. I thought I might find you here."

And, to her horror and confusion and crushing disappointment, she realized that Giles was standing by the table.

"Giles!" She felt Paul's hand release hers, with abrupt finality. "Wh—what on earth brings you here?"

"I had an unexpected business appointment, and your father said you'd be sure to be here or at the Central. I thought I might be in time to lunch you."

"But I forestalled you, as you see." Paul's laugh was a trifle loud.

"Yes, so I noticed. But perhaps I can join you."

And without waiting for either of them to agree or dissent, Giles drew up another chair, sat down at the table and picked up the menu-card.

It was a situation of such absurdity and such horrible embarrassment that Margaret felt she must surely be in some dreadful dream. But there was something too real and inescapable about the man sitting between her and Paul for her to pursue the dream theory for any length of time.

He sat there, abominably at his ease. Having chosen and ordered his meal, he chatted easily about her purchases and her meeting with his sister that afternoon. He even exchanged a few words with the suddenly silent Paul.

By every rule of the gate crasher, he should have felt completely the odd man out. But he seemed contentedly at ease, and he played the devoted fiancé with such conviction that it was Paul who seemed to be the interloper.

This, of course, was not a role to which Paul took naturally. And, in despair, Margaret realized that he was growing restive and even sulky. A tenuous line of conversation was kept going until the coffee was reached. And then she was not all surprised to hear Paul declare that he had not noticed the time, but that he must now go immediately, to keep an early afternoon appointment.

There was a polite dispute between the men about the bill, since each seemed to want to pay for her lunch, but it ended very firmly in her being Giles's guest, she noticed annoyedly. Then Paul bade her a fairly self-possessed goodbye, to which she managed to reply with a ghost of a smile.

A moment or two later he was gone, and she was sitting alone with Giles, in a silence which seemed to stretch out into infinity.

At last, he said, with surprising gentleness, "I'm sorry."

"For what?" She flashed him an angry glance. "For spoiling everything?"

"No. For having to embarrass you by interrupting a scene which should never have taken place."

"Did you *have* to interrupt?"

"I think I did, Meg."

"Why? I'm not really any concern of yours."

"You're wearing my ring—no, don't take it off and

throw it at me," he said, forestalling the slight, angry movement she had instinctively made. "Do you think I'm going to let that damned philanderer hold hands publicly with you while——"

"He's not a philanderer!"

"Well, we won't argue that one. But will you answer me one question, Meg? Had you told him our engagement is not a real one?"

"No, certainly not."

"Then, to his knowledge, you were an engaged girl—and *his* girl is lying dangerously ill in hospital. Do you think his behaviour particularly admirable?"

"You don't understand!" But she was a good deal taken aback by this analysis of the case. "He's terribly worried about Hester, because I think he's beginning to guess the position. So we started to talk of something else, less distressing. We were recalling the past and—and——"

"A distressed, engaged man recalling the past has no need to hold another man's girl by the hand," was the dry retort.

"You deliberately turn everything the wrong way round, just because you hate Paul!"

"I don't hate him. I despise him."

"You mean you're jealous of him!"

From the angry sparkle in his eye, and the way his hand suddenly clenched, she knew she had hit home. And, because she was herself so sore and wretched and disappointed, she wanted to hurt him too.

"You're jealous," she repeated, "because you know I'll never feel about you as I do about him. You flatter yourself you have some sort of claim on me because I'm wearing your ring. But I don't *want* your ring—not any more. I won't hand it back to you across the table, because it's all too silly and public here. But when we get home tonight I shall return it."

"Meg, please——"

"No. I've nothing else to say to you. You just thrust

yourself upon me—upon us, and if you're hearing things you don't like that's your own fault. But I've finished now. I'm not sitting here any longer with company *not of my own choosing.*"

And, gathering up her bag and her gloves and her parcels, she rose from the table and walked out of the restaurant, without a backward glance.

She was certain that he looked after her, but he made no attempt to follow her. And the most infuriating and disturbing feature of the whole scene was that, deep down inside her, there was an illogical, inexplicable little feeling of disappointment that he did not.

CHAPTER IX

As Margaret walked up to the Haymarket, where she was to meet Maxine's bus, anger still burnt within her.

How could Giles say such ridiculous and offensive things about Paul, even if he were jealous—which he undoubtedly was? And why did he have to choose for his unwelcome interruption just that wonderful, pregnant moment when Paul had murmured, "Darling——" and she had been on the very verge of knowing what his real feelings now were?

Of course, academically speaking, Paul *had* no right to be so attentive to her if he thought her still engaged to someone else. But it was hard to blame him for that. And anyway, all he had been expressing was wistful nostalgia for happiness past but not, perhaps, entirely beyond recapture. Anyone could do that, surely, without the ugly word "philanderer" coming into it. Giles was too ready with his censure and criticism where Paul was concerned, she thought indignantly. And once more she tried to whip up her anger against him.

But Margaret was growing cooler now. Even cool enough to regret the bitterness of her speech and the absurdity of her exit. For one thing, her reaction would only make Giles all the more critical of her attitude towards Paul. And for another, her desire to hurt him—which had been intense at the time—had now inexplicably evaporated.

It was possible now to think of half a dozen better ways in which she could have handled that scene. But it was too late. And the thought vexed her so much that, when she saw the Morpeth bus draw in, and Maxine descend with a smile and a wave, it was all she could do to summon an answering smile and look as though she had not a care in the world.

"Margaret, how nice!" Maxine, looking extraordinarily young and pretty, kissed her warmly. "Can you really bear to trail round juvenile departments and household stores before we settle down to a good gossip?"

"But of course! That's what I'm here for," Margaret declared, her spirits insensibly rising. For, complicated though the situation might be, with her engagement to Giles virtually broken, the fact was that the prospect of an afternoon in his sister's company was still a desirable one.

Shopping with Maxine was a singularly enjoyable experience. Like her mother, she knew exactly what she wanted. But, unlike Eileen, she was prepared to make herself very pleasant about getting it. Margaret could not help noticing that almost every penny had to be carefully considered. But Maxine did this with a sort of gusto which made it appear rather fun to have to plan and contrive.

"Does all this come naturally to you?" Margaret asked irrepressibly. "Or did you have to discipline yourself to it?"

"Does all what come naturally?" Maxine rapidly crossed a couple of items off her shopping list.

"This talent—almost enthusiasm—for planning and making do. Is it natural, or did you have to learn it with the years?"

"I've had to learn to plan and contrive," Maxine admitted with a smile. "But I never had to learn to be enthusiastic about it, because I suppose I have a natural enthusiasm for tasting whatever life has to offer."

"You're not—afraid of life at all, are you?" Margaret glanced at her curiously, almost enviously.

"No, Margaret." The other girl shook her head. "And that's the one thing I hope to be able to pass on to my children, because I think it's the basis of happiness. So many people imagine that happiness is the avoidance of unpleasant experiences or the accumulation of nice ones. It's not at all, of course. It's the ability to face tomorrow in the smiling belief that you can tackle it."

"Maxine, that's profound!" Margaret stopped in her tracks, so abruptly that a stout gentleman coming along behind almost cannoned into her, to his great annoyance.

"Is it?" Maxine shrugged. "But it's obvious. None of us can decide what life will bring, but all of us can decide how to meet it."

"Does Giles think that way too?" Margaret asked, with sudden uncontrollable curiosity, as she began to walk slowly onwards.

"I don't know." Maxine flashed a quick glance at the serious face of the girl her brother was to marry. "You'd better ask him. You're the one who's going to live with him, and it's you who will be affected by his outlook."

Margaret made no answer to this, because the temptation to say she was not the one who was going to live with Giles was almost irresistible. And then, to her mingled relief and disappointment, Maxine changed the subject entirely, and they talked of minor matters during the rest of the shopping spree.

Only when they were seated later at tea did Maxine look thoughtfully once more at her stepsister and inquire:

"Is everything all right with you and your affairs, Margaret?"

"How do you mean?" Margaret looked slightly put out.

"I don't know," Maxine confessed. "I couldn't put my finger on it. I just thought you looked a bit—harassed and uncertain. Is Mother being difficult?"

"Not more so than usual."

The candour of that made the other girl laugh. But then she went on, in such a matter-of-fact sort of tone that it was impossible to be offended:

"Then have you and Giles quarrelled?"

There was a slight silence. Then Margaret said, "How did you guess?"

"By thinking of myself in the same position," was the prompt reply. "I also was engaged once, you know——"

Maxine smiled—"and when one's terribly in love with someone——"

"But I'm not," Margaret burst out. "At least—not with Giles."

And then she was dumb at her own ill-judged admission.

For a long moment Maxine sat digesting that in silence, and it occurred to Margaret that possibly she was finding some difficulty in facing what *this* afternoon had brought in the smiling belief that she could tackle it.

Finally, Maxine said, "You mean there's someone else?"

"Yes."

"Quite recently, or did you take Giles on the rebound?"

"It's not recent. It started—quite a long time ago. But I didn't take Giles on the rebound. He—knew all along."

"What did Giles know all along?" inquired Maxine, understandably finding this a bit obscure.

And then it all came tumbling out. The story that Margaret had really wanted to tell her from the beginning, because with Maxine it seemed ridiculous to be acting on false pretences. Only one had not wanted to hurt or disappoint her, and at the time silence had seemed best. Now it just seemed cowardly and foolish, and she would not have blamed the other girl if she had said so. At the end, however, Maxine merely said:

"I must say you had pretty bad luck as well as everything else."

"It must all sound rather feeble to you," Margaret admitted. "You'd never have got caught in such a web, would you?"

"I?" Maxine looked surprised. "No, of course not. But then I'm a different kind of person. You can't blame people for the type they are, any more than for the colour of their hair. I suppose that, all those years when you had to be a buffer-state in your family, you were perpetually balancing one difficulty against another, and often you must have temporized and just waited for things to improve. You simply pursued the course you were used to, I guess."

"Yes," said Margaret humbly. "And look where it's landed me!"

"And Giles," added the other girl softly.

"I know." Margaret stirred unhappily in her seat. "But people do get over these things, Maxine."

"Of course. You might even get over Paul."

"Oh, I don't know about that!" Margaret was not willing to view that as a possibility.

"You would have had to do so if he had married Hester. You may still have to, if he does marry her."

"He won't marry her." Margaret spoke almost fiercely. "John is going to marry Hester. I'm nearly as sure of it as he is."

"In which case you think Paul will come back to you?"

"Of course."

"There isn't really an 'of course' about it," Maxine said, but impersonally, which made it difficult to argue hotly.

"Maxine, he was on the verge of saying something about—about his real feelings for me when Giles interrupted. If only he had waited just five minutes longer!"

"It's asking a lot of any man that he should take his time when someone else is holding his girl by the hand and making eyes at her," said Maxine; but still in that curiously impersonal way, as though they were discussing just anyone, instead of the man she loved best in the world, next to her husband.

This had the effect, of course, of making Margaret much less angry with Giles, and much more anxious to do him justice.

"Maxine, I don't want to hurt Giles——" she began.

"You can't help it, if he loves you and you love someone else," replied Maxine practically. "But, before you hurt him too much, you want to make certain of your own feelings."

"I *am* certain of my own feelings," Margaret retorted quickly. "I love Paul."

"And if you can't have him, you just don't want anyone?"

"Ye—es, that right."

"Then I think you should break with Giles now. He's much too nice to be anyone's stop-gap."

That was what Pen had said—only in different words! And the truth of the statement was so clear that Margaret's tone was genuinely contrite as she said:

"I know. I don't quite understand how I ever let him become involved in that position."

"And I don't know how he came to allow it himself," Maxine countered dryly. "It isn't like him at all to allow circumstances to overtake him. I suppose——" again she looked reflectively at Margaret—"he must have been very much in love with you even when he first got involved."

"Oh, I don't think so!" Margaret was unaccountably dismayed at such an idea. "He just got—pushed from one awkward situation to another, as I did."

"That doesn't sound like Giles to me," Maxine said, but not argumentatively, and Margaret let the subject drop.

Conversation had suddenly become very difficult. Not because of any resentment on the part of either, but because absolutely everything had been said and now— Margaret faced the unpalatable truth with reluctance— the time had come for action.

"I shall break it off with him when I go home tonight," she said finally. "I told him I was going to. But that was when I was in a temper. I'm not in a temper any more. I—I just can't go on being so unfair to him."

"Regardless of Paul's reaction?"

"How do you mean?" Margaret's eyes widened.

"Well, my dear, if Paul isn't seriously interested in you and finds you desirable simply because you happen to belong to someone else—no, don't protest; some men are like that you know—then, of course, he'll start to do some shrewd guessing about your sensationally short engagement. He can hardly fail to guess that it was bogus, and merely invented to save your pride over his desertion. Wasn't that what you've been dreading, and planning to avoid all along?"

"It doesn't—seem so—important now," Margaret said slowly.

"Because you're sure of Paul?"

"No." It took an effort to admit that, but she was determined to be honest now, even with herself. "Because, as you say, Giles is too nice to be used as someone's stop-gap."

Maxine gave that quick, brilliant smile of hers and patted Margaret's hand.

"Good luck," she said briefly. "And now I must go, dear. I've already left it later than I meant to."

It was raining when they came out of the tea-place, and as they hurried to the Haymarket to catch their respective buses, there was a chill in the air and the cold drops stung their cheeks. Nothing could have been more different from the radiant morning when Paul had come back into her life, Margaret thought sadly, and it was difficult not to feel that, in some strange and depressing way, the party was over.

All the talk and discussion, all the smiling and guessing had been done. Now she had to go home in the rain and deal bravely with as awkward a situation as one could imagine.

Maxine kissed her goodbye, but a trifle absently, Margaret felt, as though her thoughts were already running ahead to her happy home and family. Lucky Maxine, with all her problems behind her!

Only, of course, if all the present difficulties culminated in reunion with Paul, the price would be a small one to pay.

And this was what Margaret kept on telling herself, as she sat in the front seat of the bus and watched the rain bounce off the road, all the way home.

When she first came into the house, Margaret thought there was no one in. It was all so quiet. But when she went through into the drawing-room at the back of the house, there was Eileen, sitting by a welcome fire, in an attitude of pensive elegance.

She looked up as Margaret came in, and it was obvious to anyone who knew her well that she was waiting for an audience. Her eyes sparkled with malice though her lips curled in a smile, as she exclaimed :

"Well, this is a nice state of things, I must say!"

Margaret's heart skipped a couple of beats. Surely Giles had not come home and told *Eileen* of their quarrel!

But her stepmother's next words reassured her on that point, even while they roused fresh emotion.

"I always *knew* there was something funny about John haunting the hospital and pestering that poor girl and her parents," Eileen went on bitterly. "But whatever your father says, I think it's very poor behaviour to try to influence a girl when she's sick. The other fellow is nothing to me, but I must say my sympathies are with him."

Margaret came slowly forward and sat down in the chair on the other side of the fireplace.

"Do you mind telling me what you're talking about, Eileen?" she said very coolly.

"Why, your brother John, and Hester Graham. Haven't you heard? Oh, no, of course, you've been away all day in Newcastle, enjoying yourself——" the faint implication was that she herself had been working her fingers to the bone in Margaret's absence. "Apparently, he's so worked on her while she has been ill and weak that she has decided she doesn't want to marry her fiancé after all, but your brother John instead. Though no one, of course, could describe him as much of a catch," Eileen added, as a spiteful little afterthought.

"Then presumably it must be a case of real feeling," retorted Margaret coldly. "I don't know why you should talk as though John has done something underhand. Hester is a perfectly free agent, and John has been seeing her with the utmost approval of her parents. People do change their minds about these things sometimes. I suppose Hester just changed hers."

"At such short notice?" Eileen thrust out her underlip scornfully. "Why, she hadn't been engaged to this other fellow for more than a matter of weeks. Hardly more than a day or two longer than you."

"That's true," murmured Margaret, feeling profoundly uncomfortable.

"I hope *you* wouldn't take the same irresponsible view of things!" Eileen shot a quick glance at Margaret. "I shouldn't like to think of my son at the mercy of some girl who felt she could play fast and loose with him—— Well," she demanded impatiently, as Margaret remained stonily silent, "why don't you say something?"

"I don't know what to say, Eileen." Margaret was goaded into some sort of reply. "I don't know how to conduct this sort of conversation. You seem determined to find fault with John and, by some sort of extension, with me too. I imagine that anything I could say would only make matters worse."

"Don't be so absurd!" Eileen laughed and tossed her head slightly. "You're just trying to make me out unreasonable, and that simply won't do. I'm one of the most reasonable of women. Your father says so. You shouldn't be so ready to pick quarrels, Margaret. It isn't becoming in a girl of your age. But I suppose the fact is that you're just a tiny bit jealous of Giles's devotion for me."

At this blatant reversal of the truth, Margaret was hard put to it to keep her temper. But she merely said:

"I'm not jealous, Eileen." And then unfortunately could not refrain from adding, "But it has sometimes occurred to me that you might be. So perhaps it would be better if——"

"*I*? Jealous of *you*?" Eileen laughed furiously. "My dear, how little you know me—or Giles either—if you can think that. Why, no one—literally no one—could come between me and him. I have no need to be afraid of anyone on that score. Least of all of an insignificant, scheming little nobody like you. Ever since I came here——"

Margaret got up, aware that no defence would serve her against the fury of Eileen's pent-up jealousy and spite. But, even as she turned to go, someone else spoke up for her.

"That will do, Mother," Giles's voice said, coolly, from the doorway. "I won't have you say such things of Margaret."

"I was provoked," wailed Eileen, allowing the tears to well into her eyes and spill effectively down her cheeks.

"I can't help that. Even if it were the case—which I doubt—what you said was inexcusable."

"Oh, Giles, how c-can you speak to me like that? You know how easily upset——"

"Margaret is the girl I love," Giles went on unequivocally, "and any defence of her—against you or anyone else—is my business." And, putting his arm reassuringly round Margaret, he drew her slightly against him.

Not until then did she realize quite how shaken she had been by Eileen's sudden attack. And, whatever the new relationship she was determined to impose upon them, she was glad in that moment to lean against him while the sick, angry trembling subsided.

Eileen was dabbing at her eyes now, and uttering small, pathetic sounds. But for once, Giles showed no sympathy.

"Pull yourself together, Mother, and stop being silly," he said bracingly. "We all let our tempers get the better of us occasionally. The only thing is to apologize and try to forget it."

In the slight silence which followed this admirable advice it became obvious that no apologies were forthcoming from Eileen. And so, with his arm still round Margaret, he turned away and led her out of the room.

"I'm sorry," he said briefly, when they reached the hall. "I'm afraid it was a bad scene I interrupted, wasn't it?"

"Not very nice. But the whole situation is so totally

false and—and absurd by now that I can't really blame anyone but myself." Margaret clasped and unclasped her hands nervously. "Come into the study, Giles. I must talk to you."

He came, though reluctantly, she saw. And she supposed he was still remembering the note on which they had parted that afternoon.

"Listen, Giles," she began breathlessly, "this has nothing to do with what happened this afternoon. I was angry when I walked out on you, but I'm not angry any more. I'm ashamed of myself. I've had time to think things over, and I realize that the person who's caused all this trouble is myself——"

"Nonsense," he interrupted crisply, but she went on.

"I should never have involved you in this situation; never have accepted your generous offer to help me out of the original dilemma. I've made an enemy of your mother, put you in an impossible position and—and finally——" she looked down at her hands, now tightly clasped together again—"I've hurt you abominably."

"I can take it." She thought from his tone that he was actually amused and, glancing up quickly, she saw that he was smiling. "I'm tough, you know," he assured her.

"But not as tough as that! Anyway, I'm not sure that you're really tough at all," Margaret said earnestly. "If you were, you couldn't be so sensitive about other people's feelings, and when I think——"

"Dear, you can't make a sensitive plant out of me," he told her tenderly and, laughing a little, he took the tightly clasped hands in his. "It wasn't your fault that I fell in love with you—unless being your darling self is your own fault. And if anyone had to help you out of this particular spot of bother, do you really suppose I would have had anyone but myself do it?"

"That isn't the *point*!" But, almost without knowing it, she had turned her hands and clasped his tightly, and found something infinitely comforting in the contact. "I feel so—awful about it all. For so long I've thought of nothing but *my* position, *my* reactions. And all the time it must have been the most horrible position for you. And you've never once lost your temper. But it can't go on this way. I've used you long enough. We've got to make an end of——"

"Is this your special way of chucking my ring back at me?" he inquired.

"Not *chucking* it back, Giles! I'm past that silly spurt of temper. But I want you to take it back and for us——" she was already trying to get her ring off her finger, but he stopped her.

"Don't, dear—please. Not at this moment, of all moments. How are we going to tell Mother, on top of this idiotic scene, that we're breaking our engagement?"

"It couldn't be a worse time, I know," she admitted unhappily. "But we can't go on like this. It's grossly unfair to you and——"

"Don't you think that's for me to decide? And do you really think I'm going to find the situation any more attractive by adding the first-class sensation of a dramatically broken engagement to it?"

"Another broken engagement, you mean," she murmured.

"What's that?" He glanced at her quickly. "What other one?"

"Oh, you don't know, I see. That's how the scene with Eileen started. She was telling me that Hester had broken her engagement to—to Paul, and is going to marry John. They've come out into the open about it, it seems."

He let her hands go at that, and slowly thrust his into his pockets.

"I—see." He stared at the ground. "So Paul is free. And that's why you're so desperately anxious to be free too."

"No," Margaret said quickly. "No, that's not the primary reason." And, to her surprise, she realized that, somehow, that was true. "Anything that—happens with Paul is incidental to what we're discussing. I'm just sick and ashamed at the way I've exploited you, and I want us to be truthful about things and dissolve this bogus engagement, which can't mean anything but pain and—and humiliation for you."

"You'd be surprised." He grinned at her boyishly. "I've enjoyed quite a lot of it. And, touched though I am by your anxiety for my wounded feelings, my choice is that we go on with this until——"

"I can't! I feel so awful—and spineless—and guilty ——" And suddenly she began to cry.

"Meg dear!" He was terribly taken aback. But then he put his arms round her and held her close. "Look, sweetheart, you mustn't *cry* about it. Truly, you're being absurdly tender-hearted. There always has to be a loser in these things, you know. Stop trying to tear yourself in half and please everyone. You've had to do that too long for the family, and I certainly won't have you doing it over me and Paul. I went into this with my eyes open, and if I fell in love with you—that's my affair. If you want to be free on account of Paul——"

"I don't!" she whispered, illogically but emphatically. "I just want to consider *you* for once."

"Well, consider me, then." He laughed and kissed the tip of her ear. "And spare me the most complicated explanations which I should certainly have to make, if we chose to announce two broken engagements in the family circle at this moment. Timing can make an awful difference, Meg. If you want my advice—or really feel like studying my wishes—you'll let it ride for just a bit longer."

"You—mean that?" Absently she twisted his beautiful ring on her finger, but not with any effort to take it off.

"Absolutely."

"It seems so—weak," she objected, trying to resist the delicious sensation of relief which began to creep over her at the thought of postponing the crisis, after all.

"You'll let me decide this," he told her firmly. "Let the

family get used to the shake-up over John and Hester, and, in our own time, we'll make our announcement."

She knew she ought not to let him talk her into this. She knew she was tempting fate to present her with fresh complications. But, with his arm round her and his voice persuasively offering her a reprieve, she simply had not the resolution to insist on the hard course. And in any case, if this delay were indeed what he wanted, could she not at least allow him this small indulgence?

"Giles, if you mean this honestly—and it's not some further quixotic notion about helping me——"

"Cross my heart, this is really what I want. And anyway, I'm not at all quixotic."

"I think you are," she said earnestly. "I think that's just what you are. Quixotic and a darling and much, much too good for the way I've used you—and I'm a beast."

And she reached up and kissed him with such warmth and fervour that he gave a pleased, astonished laugh and, holding her close, he kissed her in return so tenderly that Penelope, coming into the room at that moment, stopped dead and looked at them in astonishment.

"Goodness," she observed, with innocent candour, "that's the first time I've seen you kiss each other as though you really were in love."

"Pen, don't be absurd," exclaimed Margaret.

But Giles merely smiled thoughtfully and said, "A profound observation from a close observer. What's the news?"

"Haven't you heard?" Penelope was nothing loth to give the full budget. "Hester Graham isn't going to marry that brash, self-satisfied Paul Freemantle, after all. She's going to marry our John, and a much better bargain she's got there, if you ask me," added John's youngest sister, who was deeply prejudiced where he was concerned.

"I'm absolutely with you there, Pen," Giles agreed gravely.

"And the odd thing is," went on Penelope, pleased to

have her opinion supported, "that Father's tickled pink about it. I don't think John's ever done anything that's pleased him more. I heard him talking about making a settlement and seeing that his land was extended, and all about Hester being a girl any father-in-law would be glad to see properly provided for. And John said something about Hester's father wanting to help them too, and——"

"Were you listening at the door?" inquired Margaret flatly.

"Not actually *at* the door. Just inside it," explained Penelope, with a nice distinction of meaning. "They could have seen me quite easily, if they'd liked to look, but they were too busy discussing things to notice me, I guess. And anyway, it was all *nice* news and about making people happy, so it doesn't really matter if I eavesdropped, does it?"

Margaret said something about the principle of the thing, but Giles gave it as his opinion that it didn't matter in this particular case, and added that everything seemed remarkably satisfactory.

"Except for poor Paul Freemantle, of course," said Penelope, with belated sympathy. "But I expect he'll soon get himself another nice girl. He's that sort, isn't he?"

To this Margaret had absolutely no answer ready. But Giles rubbed his chin thoughtfully and said:

"I think that's how I'd describe him too. But then I'm not exactly unprejudiced."

"Aren't you?" Penelope immediately looked interested. But fortunately, before she could inquire into the absorbing subject of Giles's prejudices, Gloria sounded the dinner gong imperiously, and everyone converged on the dining-room.

There was, Margaret saw, no doubt about her father's satisfaction or her brother's quiet radiance. And, in her husband's presence, even Eileen refrained from acid comment and contrived to give an impression of sharing in everyone's satisfaction. She did just allow herself to observe that it seemed a teeny-weeny bit unfair to have stolen a march on that poor Paul Freemantle, when he was away abroad on an assignment. But, as no one offered to argue or develop this view, the subject was allowed to lapse.

It was Penelope, as usual, who launched into elaborate planning, and she almost had the banns up before they reached the sweet. Then a fresh and delightful idea struck her.

"Don't you think it would be lovely if we made it a *double* wedding?" she exclaimed. "I mean if Meg and Giles got married the same day as John and Hester."

"Certainly not!" Eileen, who detested anything which gave reality to her son's impending marriage, spoke before Margaret could find her voice. "I don't think double weddings are *ever* a success. You can't have two people in the centre of a really good picture. I mean two identical people. Of course——" she smiled winningly at Giles—"you do have to have the bride as well as the bridegroom."

"Most people would put that the other way round, Mother," replied Giles, but good-humouredly, to show that she was no longer under a cloud.

"I couldn't agree with Eileen more," said Margaret, for once able to find herself in something like harmony with her stepmother. "I'm sure I should hate to share anyone else's wedding day. Besides, Pen," she added, with inspiration, "you wouldn't want to miss a second chance of being bridesmaid, would you?"

"Of course not! I forgot that!" Immediately the idea of the double wedding was dismissed. "And of course, Elinor will be the grown-up bridesmaid, won't she, and she loves to have a reason for wearing pretty clothes and —my goodness! She doesn't know yet, does she? She *will* be thrilled."

"She does know." John gave his little sister a smile. "She was the first person I told, by telephone."

"And was she pleased?"

"Very pleased."

"I hardly think anyone could be other than pleased," put in Mr. Masters, with characteristic unawareness of any view but his own, even if the embodiment of opposition was sitting beside him. Eileen smiled thinly, and listened with an air of tolerance while the chorus of mutual satisfaction broke out again.

It was considerably later that evening—when Margaret had had time to re-examine her own equivocal position with some dissatisfaction—that she was summoned to the telephone.

As she hastened to answer Gloria's economical announcement of, "Phone. For you," she could not entirely suppress a sudden, eager hope that, for some reason, Paul was calling her up. But it was Elinor's voice at the other end of the wire.

"Meg? Oh, I wish I were at home with you all this evening. It's wonderful news about John and Hester, isn't it? And pretty important for you, too, because now Paul——"

"Yes, yes—I know what you mean," interrupted Margaret hastily, with the obscure feeling that even on the telephone one must not be too frank about unbidden hopes.

"Of course you know," responded Elinor, with uninhibited emphasis. "And that's really why I'm phoning you. Meg, you must come here on Friday and stay overnight with me. The Felsons—very nice people who've been wonderfully kind to me—are giving a supper-dance, and you're invited too. They have a gorgeous house, overlooking the Town Moor. And, Meg, the vital thing is that Paul Freemantle will almost certainly be there. It couldn't be better timed. You *will* manage it, won't you?"

CHAPTER X

Just as Elinor uttered the magic name Paul Freemantle, Giles happened to cross the hall, and immediately Margaret was overcome by an agitated and illogical feeling of guilt. So much so that, by the time Elinor had completed her speech with the energetic injunction that Margaret should make all haste to meet Paul as soon as possible, a sort of shy reluctance had descended upon her.

"Elinor, I'll—I'll have to think about it," she was surprised to hear herself explain. "I mean—Friday's a bit awkward. I'm often rather late at the Works, and——"

"What do you *mean*?" Elinor sounded both incredulouse and impatient. "This is important. At least, it's important if you're still interested in Paul Freemantle. Aren't you interested any more?"

"Of course!" Margaret assured her hastily. "In fact——"

"Well then, make it your business to get away in good time. Surely you can do that, for goodness' sake! What's the good of being the boss's daughter if you can't arrange a little thing like that? And even if you did have to stay a bit late, someone could drive you in. Giles would, I suppose."

"I couldn't possibly ask Giles to drive me," exclaimed Margaret, somehow scandalized at the idea of asking Giles to convey her to her rendezvous with his rival.

But, to her dismay, Giles's voice said, "Of course you could. Where do you want to be driven?"

And, turning sharply, she saw that he was standing by the hall table, looking up something in the telephone directory.

"Oh, Giles, I didn't realize you were still there!"

"Sorry. I'm just going, anyway." He scribbled down a number and closed the directory "You can ask me to drive you wherever you like. I'll manage it somehow."

"Th—thank you," she murmured uncomfortably, as she watched his retreating back, while Elinor's voice rattled on impatiently in her ears.

"Are you still there?" demanded Elinor suddenly.

"Yes. I was just talking to—to Giles. He happened to come into the hall."

"Oh, I see. Well, anyway, you'll come on Friday, won't you, Meg? I've gone to quite a lot of trouble to get you this invitation, and I thought you'd be delighted."

"I *am* delighted," Margaret insisted remorsefully. "And of course I'll come. It was just that—at first—I thought——"

She stopped, unable to continue with any sensible account of what she had thought.

"What did you think?" inquired Elinor exactly.

"Oh, things have become so much more difficult and——"

"More *difficult?*" Elinor sounded astonished again. "I should have thought everything had been immensely simplified by the Hester-John engagement."

"Well, in some ways—yes."

"In what way haven't they been simplified?" Elinor wanted to know, with the persistence of an elder sister clarifying a situation she found unnecessarily obscure.

"I'll explain when I see you," cried Margaret, quite unable to continue this conversation. "And thanks a million for the invitation, Elinor. I'll be with you on Friday—the day after tomorrow—just as soon as I can."

She rang off then, and escaped upstairs to her own room, not only to avoid any further questions from Giles, but also because she felt she had to do something about disentangling her own ideas about this unexpected development.

This, however, proved more difficult than she could have supposed. She sat by her bedroom window, looking out over the Tyne Valley, which lay there in the moonlight like a glorious study in black and silver.

Of course she was enraptured at the thought of seeing Paul again. And seeing him in circumstances which would mean neither unwelcome observation nor interruption. At last—at last, she would know how he really felt, just what he had been going to add to that softly-breathed, "Darling——" And, because he would be fresh from the pain and disappointment of his broken engagement, he would be ready for the sympathy and understanding which she longed to lavish upon him.

It simply could not have been better timed. The barriers would be down. They could speak frankly to each other at last. And everything which had happened in the recent disastrous weeks would be as though it had never happened. The engagement with Hester was already a thing of the past. The so-called engagement to Giles——

She stopped there, and bit her lip.

If *only* she need not hurt Giles, who had been so incredibly good to her! He had been so understanding and helpful and—gay about it all. Just as though it were something that he could enjoy, instead of something which must have wrung his heart very often.

"You can't help hurting him," Maxine had said, "if he loves you, and you love someone else."

So true—so true! But she shrank from administering the final blow. Particularly now, when they had arrived at such a real—almost affectionate—understanding.

Anyway, there could be no question of his actually driving her into Newcastle on the journey which was to mean her reunion with Paul. That at least she must avoid.

And with this thought in mind, Margaret went downstairs to give only the briefest and most general goodnight. Then she hurried upstairs again, in the hope that, by morning, he would have forgotten about that half-heard suggestion in the hall.

Vain hope, however. Giles seemed incapable of forgetting anything about herself. And, on the way to the Works the next morning, he inquired:

"Where do you want me to drive you on Friday, Meg?"

"On Friday? Nowhere, thanks. I can manage quite easily."

"What's happening on Friday?" inquired her father, who was also in the car.

"Meg's going to Newcastle to stay the night with Elinor," explained Penelope, who was having her customary lift to school and was, as usual, pleased to show herself well-informed about everything. "I heard you telling Gloria you wouldn't be home and that you were going to town to stay with Elinor," she added to her sister.

"There's a supper-dance, given by friends of Elinor's," Margaret explained hastily, making a virtue of necessity. "Rather a special affair, from what Elinor said."

"Full evening?" inquired Penelope, sucking in her cheeks appreciatively.

"I expect so."

"Then you'll be taking quite a large case," Giles observed practically. "You won't want to go by bus. I'll drive you in, naturally."

"It isn't necessary——" Margaret began. But her father created a rather unwelcome diversion by inquiring:

"Didn't they invite Giles too? Rather odd, surely, to ask an engaged girl without her fiancé."

"The original invitation was for Elinor," Margaret said desperately. "I was just a sort of extension of it."

"I don't understand," said her father, with the obtuse air he usually assumed when he was pushing through a clever business deal. "I should have thought that, if they extended the invitation at all, the natural thing would have been to include you *and* your fiancé."

"They may have had too many men already," suggested Margaret, a trifle wildly.

"No party ever has too many men. Only too many girls," put in Penelope sagely.

But fortunately, at that moment, they came in sight of

the school gates, and Penelope let out a loud, "Yoo-hoo!" of welcome to Dorothy Emms who had, for once, preceded her. And, as she was decanted from the car, and fell upon Dorothy with the interest and rapture which a separation of mere hours seems to engender at that age, Giles said coolly and finally:

"Well, it doesn't matter, anyway. If the invitation is a good one and Meg wants to accept it, that's perfectly all right, of course. But I'll drive you in, my dear. I'm not having you haul a heavy case on and off buses."

Short of attaching disproportionate importance to the incident, Margaret simply had to let that arrangement stand. And so, the following evening, Giles collected her and her case from the office at the Works and, accompanied by the slightly envious good wishes of her colleagues (for Giles was a great favourite with all the other girls in the office) Margaret drove away to Newcastle, to meet Paul again.

Oppressed by an indefinable sensation of guilt and deceit, she remained very silent during the first part of the drive. Then Giles asked, with a sort of idle curiosity:

"Why were you so determined not to let me drive you in tonight, Meg?"

"I—wasn't. At least—well, I suppose I felt a bit mean, going to this dance w—without you."

"Whatever for?" He glanced at her in genuine surprise. "You don't think my feelings are so easily hurt, do you?"

"No." At least, she wouldn't have expected him to show it, if they had been.

"Is it a very special dance?"

She should have answered promptly, and yet casually. But she hesitated for a fatal moment. And suddenly, without even looking at him, she knew that he had jumped to the right conclusion.

"Are you going to see Paul Freemantle, Meg?"

"He—he may be at the dance."

"I see. Did you and he arrange it that way?"

"No. He doesn't even know I'm coming."

"But that was why you didn't want me to drive you to town? You thought I might—meet him?"

"Oh, no! No I don't think there's any likelihood of that happening. I just thought it was—mean to use you and your car when I was going to see him." ·

To her surprise, he laughed softly at that, and said, "You are adorable."

She could not imagine why he should think that of her at just that moment. Nor could she imagine why the tears suddenly came into her eyes. If she could have steadied her voice, she would have told him that she felt anything but adorable. That in fact, in some obscure way, she felt mean. But somehow the words would not come. And they drove the rest of the way in silence.

When they arrived at Elinor's flat—in one of the attractive old converted houses on the Jesmond side of Newcastle—he lifted Margaret's case from the car and set it beside her at the front door. Then, smiling, he bent his head and kissed her.

"Have a good time, sweet," he said.

Then he returned to the car and drove off, just as Elinor opened the door.

"Hello, you are in good time!" she exclaimed, as she eagerly drew her sister into the house. And then— "What's the matter? You look as though you're going to cry or something."

Margaret shook her head.

"It's all right. I'm not going to cry. I was just a—a bit upset."

"About what? Oh," said Elinor in sudden comprehension, "was that Giles who just drove away?"

"Yes." Margaret followed her sister upstairs and into her first-floor flat.

"Oh, dear! Did he guess the real situation and turn nasty?"

"No. He guessed the real situation and was perfectly s—sweet and generous about it. And that's why I could just sit down and howl, if it wouldn't be such a silly thing to do."

"It would be a perfectly idiotic thing to do," Elinor assured her briskly. "This ought to be nearly the happiest evening of your life, if things work out as we hope. I'm sorry about poor old Giles, if he really is being decent about things. But it just can't be helped. There always has to be a loser in these matters and——"

"Oh, Elinor! That was what *he* said," exclaimed Margaret unhappily.

"He did? Well, that was handsome of him," her sister conceded. "But perfectly realistic too, of course. Cheer up, Meg. You're going to see your true love this evening, in about the most favourable circumstances any girl could ask. You needn't look as though you'd—oh, I don't know what—just said farewell to your best friend."

"Why do you put it *that* way?" cried Margaret, on a note of sudden pain.

"What way?" Elinor looked surprised. "It's just a figure of speech. Oh, you mean because it's Giles you've just said goodbye to. I didn't mean it literally, you silly. And anyway, *is* he your best friend?"

For quite a long moment Margaret was silent. Then she said, sombrely, "I doubt if I'll ever have a better."

"Well, that's splendid." Elinor was determinedly cheerful. "It's nice to know you've got someone like that in the family. He's still your stepbrother, after all. Mine too, though I never think of him that way. And once he's not living any longer under the same roof, you won't feel so embarrassed. What's come of that scheme of his for having a place of his own, by the way? I thought it was all fixed."

"I suppose he's still going ahead with it. In fact—yes. I'm sure he is. There was a lot of reconstruction and alteration to be done to the place, though."

"Did you and he pretend it was where you intended to set up married life?" Elinor inquired, with uninhibited curiosity.

"We—didn't go into that," Margaret said hastily.

"Didn't you really? I should have thought Eileen would have wanted it all discussed in detail."

"No," Margaret replied almost curtly. "She hates the mention of anything which gives reality to the position."

"But she knew about the house—cottage—whatever it is?"

"She knew we had looked at the place together," Margaret conceded reluctantly. "At the time when Giles was supposed to be—in fact, *was*—looking for a bachelor place of his own."

"Oh, it was only suitable for one person, you mean? It wouldn't have done for two people just starting married life together?"

"It would have done b—beautifully for that," Margaret said, and again she found herself ridiculously and inexplicably near tears.

Elinor glanced at her quickly.

"You're overwrought, for some reason or other," she observed practically. "You probably need a cup of tea and something to eat. You won't have had anything since lunch. Sit down by the fire and be comfortable, and I'll see to everything. I expect you're terribly excited and anxious, really, over the prospect of seeing Paul again."

"I daresay," agreed Margaret submissively. And she was glad to sit by the fire and have Elinor whisking about, playing hostess in her own domain with a good deal of pleasure.

"When did you last see him?" Elinor inquired presently. "Not since the day you told him you were engaged to Giles, I suppose?"

"Oh, no! I ran in to him outside Fenwicks a day or two ago. In fact, I—had lunch with him. Just before the—the break with Hester was announced."

"You don't say!" Elinor looked intrigued. "And how did he seem? Was there anything to suggest coming events? Was he—preoccupied or anything?"

"He told me he was worried about Hester, and her friendship with John."

"Did he, indeed? And how did you deal with that?"

"I—sympathized, of course, without specifying any views of my own. Then we talked about other things——"

"What other things?" Elinor wanted to know.

"The—past, mostly. In a nostalgic sort of way. And then Giles came in and interrupted."

"Oh, no!" Elinor sounded personally affronted. "How maddening! How far had Paul got? I mean— what was he saying when Giles interrupted?"

"He was saying, 'Darling——'," said Margaret. And she smiled suddenly. For, after all, it was ridiculous not to take heart and rejoice over the fact that she and Paul had already had time to draw much closer.

"He was? Oh, Meg, then it's all plain sailing from here," declared Elinor, openly delighted on her sister's behalf. "I've heard, by the way, that he's coming to-night for certain. And—you know what I think? I think you should take off that ring you're wearing, here and now." She pointed to Giles's beautiful ring. "In the circumstances, it's all wrong to meet Paul still wearing another man's ring."

"Oh, I couldn't do that!" Margaret instinctively put a protective hand over Giles's ring.

"Why not?" Elinor looked surprised.

"Well, I just couldn't! It wouldn't be fair—right—I mean. I should feel a beast, when Giles has been so generous and understanding, if I took off his ring the moment his back was turned."

"I never heard anything so silly and illogical! You're not really engaged to Giles, and he knows that perfectly well," Elinor pointed out. "What's the magic quality attached to wearing his ring, for goodness' sake?"

Margaret winced unexpectedly at this query, though she hardly knew why.

"I'm not taking off Giles's ring without telling him first," she said obstinately.

"Well, why didn't you think of it beforehand and tell him, if he's generous and understanding?" inquired Elinor impatiently.

"I don't know. But I'm not doing it now, without his knowing," Margaret insisted.

"Well, have it your own way. But I think you're a chump," said Elinor good-humouredly. "Anyway, I suppose all this will be quite academic by the time this evening's over," she added cheerfully. "Once Paul has declared himself——"

"But he hasn't yet!" cried Margaret sharply.

"He will," Elinor prophesied confidently.

"He may not. You just don't know," argued Margaret, overwhelmed by a queer sort of panic which she could not have explained. "Don't say that sort of thing."

"Why not? Are you superstitious or something?" Elinor looked amused. "You never used to be. But if you're afraid of my breaking your luck, I won't say any more."

It had nothing to do with being superstitious or fear of breaking her luck, Margaret knew. But then she could not have identified the real reason for her sharp protest, either. So she was silent, leaving Elinor to think what she liked. And presently she was relieved to hear her sister say

"It's about time we got ready. Hugh Felson is coming for us about seven-thirty."

After that, most of their conversation turned on their dresses and their preparations.

Both girls were good-looking, but Elinor was the sophisticated, truly elegant one of the two. Margaret, however, had a very individual charm of her own, and the sea-blue chiffon dress she had chosen was almost exactly the colour of her eyes, and gave a special almost translucent beauty to her very white skin.

"In your way, you're quite a beauty, Meg," remarked her sister approvingly. "Add just a touch more colour to your lips—and see what these ear-rings do for you."

Margaret accepted the profferred ear-rings and put them on. And she was bound to agree that their sparkle, and the extra colour on her lips, gave a clear definition to her appearance which added distinction to the charm.

"Perfect," Elinor declared. "I only hope Giles thinks so too."

"*Giles?*"

"Paul, I mean. Sorry, a slip of the tongue," Elinor said carelessly. "There's no reason to look so aghast."

"I'm not looking aghast," Margaret declared defensively. And she was profoundly glad that, at that moment, there was the sound of a motor-horn outside, and Elinor exclaimed:

"There's Hugh! Come on, let's go."

They slipped on their wraps and ran downstairs, to be received very enthusiastically by Hugh Felson. He was rather older than Margaret had expected, but very personable, and it was obvious that he immensely admired her sister. To Margaret he was pleasant and welcoming, and assured her that he and his parents and sister were delighted to be having her with them that evening.

On the drive to the Felsons' home, Elinor did most of the talking. So Margaret was able to sit quietly in the back of the car, recovering her nerve and telling herself over and over again that she was to see Paul in a very short time, and that this was the evening when all doubts and anxieties were to resolve themselves in a wonderful glow of happiness and understanding.

Those happy days when she and he had first discovered that they loved each other seemed almost like another life now. Even then, of course, there had been the shadow of family responsibilities hanging over her. But all that seemed small in comparison to the emotional upheaval through which she had gone in recent weeks. Viewed from a distance, those early days with Paul seemed almost unadulterated happiness, and a return to them would surely be the answer to her fondest dreams.

Once they had spoken the longed-for words of understanding and forgiveness to each other, once they knew truly what was in each other's heart——

"Here we are," announced Elinor, as they swept into a short drive and came to a stop before a large, open, porticoed doorway, from which light was streaming.

As they entered the Felson mansion, Margaret realized that it was a much bigger place—and that the party was a much grander affair—than anything she had imagined. She thought she remembered hearing that the Felsons were big people in shipping, and it was obvious that there must be a considerable fortune behind any family that could entertain on this scale in a private house.

Mr. and Mrs. Felson proved to be pleasant, informal people who obviously regarded their children and their pursuits with great indulgence. Having welcomed the guests, they seemed to want nothing more than that they should enjoy themselves in their own chosen way.

There was quite a large ballroom at the back of the house, and a marquee had been erected in the garden, where supper was evidently to be served. At least fifty or sixty people were already there. But, before Margaret could look round for Paul, she found herself being introduced to a Felson cousin, who swept her off on to the dance floor.

It was impossible not to enjoy oneself, and nearly an hour slipped past before Margaret began to ask herself anxiously if Paul were really coming, after all.

It was difficult to pick out people individually in the crowded ballroom—and certainly this was not going to be a place where she could have a revealing and heart-to-heart talk with him. Margaret began to wonder how she was to break free of the general merry-go-round. And, when she finally found herself near her sister for a few moments, she said, softly and urgently :

"Elinor, I don't think he's come."

"Oh, yes, he has. I saw him about ten minutes ago," Elinor assured her, with a confidence that made Margaret's heart beat rapidly. "But I don't think he's dancing.

Make an excuse to slip away before the next dance. You'll probably come across him in the garden -or in one of the smaller sitting-out rooms.''

It was advice Margaret was only too willing to take. And, with an ingenuity born of determination, she eluded her very assiduous partner and slipped away from the ballroom into the quieter, less familiar part of the house.

She was not quite sure which way to go. First of all she looked into the marquee. But, although several people were there, sampling the excellent refreshments, there was no sign of Paul.

Because of the faint chill in the air, she doubted if he would be in the garden. Anyway, why should he be strolling about the garden when a party was in progress? She turned once more into the house, glanced as unobtrusively as possible into one or two of the sitting-out rooms, still without success, and then found herself before a heavy, handsome door which looked as though it might lead to a library.

Afterwards, Margaret was not quite sure why she pressed her search beyond the part of the house obviously given up to the party. But, acting on a sudden impulse she could not have defined, she put out her hand, quietly opened the heavy door and looked in.

The room was lined with books, and lighted by only one standard lamp. But a bright fire burnt on the hearth, so it was perfectly possible to see the couple who were sitting in intimate and low-toned conversation on the sofa.

The girl had been introduced to Margaret earlier in the evening as Sylvia Felson, the daughter of the house. The man was Paul.

And, even as Margaret watched, in speechless dismay, she saw Paul run his hand, lightly and caressingly, down Sylvia Fenson's bare arm, and she heard him say, in that familiar, heart-searching tone :

"Darling, how differently one would act, if one could turn back the pages.''

CHAPTER XI

Very softly, Margaret withdrew from the room and closed the door behind her.

She was trembling violently. Not so much from shock and pain, she realized surprisedly, but from rage. Sheer, red-hot rage that burned within her like a flame. But for the fact that she was a reasonably civilized being, she would have gone in now and slapped Paul across his smiling, attractive face, and told that silly deluded girl that he had said just those words to other girls. To herself for one.

Herself. Just another silly, deluded girl, in fact. A girl who had sat there in Tilleys and let him hold her hand across the table and breathe, "Darling——" and talk that guff about turning back the pages.

. How could she have been so silly as to take it all? How, having once been disillusioned by him, could she have pretty well *asked* to be duped again? No wonder Giles had interfered! No wonder he thought her a perfect idiot where Paul was concerned——

Only he had never *said* he thought her that. On the contrary, he had been infinitely patient and humorous and kind, and even said he was sorry to have to interrupt a scene which should never have taken place.

Oh, Giles! So different—so inexpressibly different from the man of straw she had been cherishing in her heart all these months. What sort of spell had made her see black as white and white as black? For long enough · now she had had the undivided love and attention of the best of men. And all she could do was push him on one side and yearn after Paul . . . who was now sitting on the library sofa, making love to Sylvia Felson because Hester Graham had escaped him and Margaret Masters was really not a good enough prospect to pursue seriously.

"I must have been mad," Margaret muttered. And as she stood there in the deserted passage leading to the Felsons' library, she ran her hands distractedly over her hair, and wondered by what possible misguided planning she could have found herself here—in this humiliating position.

The distant sound of laughter brought her to her senses with a start, and she realized that at any moment the two might come out of the library, or that someone from the opposite direction might come and find her there, dazed, aimless and without any reason for being in this part of the house.

She turned away blindly and, as she did so, sudden resolution came to her, clear-cut and determined.

I'm not staying on at this party, she thought grimly. I can't stay here and meet him and be civil to him—and know that he half guesses I'm here because of the news of his broken engagement. The idea is impossible. I'll say I'm ill.—I must find Elinor. She can make what excuses she likes——

She found Elinor with unexpected ease, just as she came from the ballroom, and hastily Margaret pulled her sister into one of the deserted smaller rooms.

"Listen, Elinor—I can't explain fully, but I'm going home. No, don't interrupt me——" as Elinor gave a short gasp—"and don't argue. You must make my excuses——"

"*What* excuses?" interjected Elinor, half angry, half scared.

"Whatever you like. Say I was faint, had a headache, or a heart attack—anything. I don't care what you say, so long as I can go. Please give me your key. I can't get home to Cromburgh tonight. And oh, I hope your friend Dulcie won't be home, because——"

"She won't," Elinor interrupted, in a dazed sort of way. "She's away until Tuesday. But you *must* tell me more than this. Are you really ill? Shall I come with you?"

"No, no. There's no need to spoil your evening. I'm perfectly all right. Just sick at my own utter stupidity."

"Oh, Meg! It's something to do with Paul, of course?"

"Yes."

"But whatever could he have said to you to make you so angry and upset? He hasn't had time——"

"It wasn't what he said to me," said Margaret distinctly, and for a moment she looked years older than Elinor. "He didn't say a word to me. It was what he was saying to someone else."

"O-oh——" A sort of dismayed comprehension began to dawn on Elinor's face. "You mean he was——?"

"Handing out the same well-worn, sentimental, *syrupy* sort of stuff that I was swallowing in great gulps only a couple of days ago. I could kick myself when I think of it."

"Meg, I've never seen you like this, never seen you so angry."

"I've never been so angry," Margaret retorted wearily. "Oh, not even so much with him as with myself. When I think—— But never mind, I simply must go if I'm going. We're lucky not to have been interrupted before now, but someone is bound to come looking for you soon. Give me your key, dear."

Rather reluctantly, Elinor produced her flat key from her evening bag and handed it over.

"How will you get home?" she wanted to know. "If you'd let someone drive you——"

"No! I couldn't make small talk with *anyone* just now. I'll get one of the servants to ring for a taxi. Or I'll get a bus or something. We're not far from the main road."

"I don't like it——" Elinor began.

"I don't like it either. In fact, I simply hate it," Margaret cut in grimly. "But I've no one to blame but myself, and all I want to do now is to get away. Don't worry. I can look after myself—now. I've come to my senses. Enjoy your evening as much as you can. I'm sorry I've half spoiled things for you, but I can't help it. I'll see you later."

And, with a light touch of affection and reassurance on her sister's arm, Margaret turned away, leaving Elinor still irresolute and worried.

It was all rather easier than she had expected.

The maid in charge of the wraps was sympathetic about her sudden, blinding headache, declaring that she too had sometimes "come over just like that". But, since she assumed that someone was naturally driving Margaret home, she did not attempt to arrange things for her.

Having waited her chance, Margaret slipped across the hall—deserted now as almost everyone had gone into the marquee for supper—and let herself out of the house.

As she ran down the lighted drive, her heart still beat heavily lest she should hear some voice querying her flight and calling her back. But again she was lucky and, in a matter of minutes, she was out in the darkened road, hurrying along—alone and blessedly anonymous.

No longer Margaret Masters, to be identified as the poor fool who had thought Paul Freemantle loved her and meant to marry her. But just a girl—any girl—in a dark evening coat, lost among the shadows and catching her breath from time to time on a stifled sob.

Anger and contempt, which had sustained her, were ebbing now. And in their place came cold waves of misery and despair.

It was over. The wonderful mirage had faded. The cherished illusions had fled. She was no longer brave and proud and resolute. All she wanted was a shoulder to cry on. And there was none within miles, for Giles must have got back to Cromburgh hours ago.

She was angry with herself for even thinking of him in this connection. But she thought of him, all the same. And she was just about to cry in real earnest when a cruising taxi appeared, and stopped at her eager hail.

It was wonderful to be safely hidden away in its darkened interior, as though completely withdrawn from

the world in which she had so sadly misjudged things
and brought such humiliation upon herself. But the
respite was brief, for very soon they arrived at Elinor's
flat, and she had to rouse herself, pay the driver, find the
key, and climb the stairs which she had descended with
such high hopes not a couple of hours ago.

But sanctuary was reached at last. She left herself into
the flat, switched on the light, put on the electric fire and,
sitting down beside it, buried her face in her hands.

In the worst moments of her distress and shame, this
had appeared to her as the very height of human
ambition. Just to sink down in relatively familiar sur-
roundings, alone, with no need to pretend or keep up
appearances or explain to anyone. Just to sit there—
alone.

But after a while this measure of relief began to seem
very meagre. Nothing could protect her from the thought
of past folly or future emptiness.

"I've lost him, of course," she said aloud. And the
strange thing was that, not even to herself, did she have
to explain that she meant Giles and not Paul.

When she had looked at Paul in the firelight, and seen
him for what he really was, it was as though something
bright but valueless had vanished at a touch. It was not
for Paul that she had stood shaking in the passage, or
run sobbing along the street. It was for the inner, growing, inescapable knowledge that tonight had put an in-
superable barrier between her and Giles.

How could she go to him now and say, "Please go on
loving me. I didn't get Paul. But I know that it's you I
want?"

What man was going to believe that, or be anything
but insulted by the suggestion?

She could hardly believe it herself, even now. Except
that there was a strange inevitability—a *rightness*—
about the thought of Giles, which was like a warm cloak
round the chill of her misery and disillusionment.

But there were no words in which one could convey

that to him. Not after she had told him that she loved Paul. Now she would have to admit—or let it gradually be assumed—that Paul had no use for her. But there it must rest. To Giles, most of all, there was no way of presenting a convincing case for a sudden change of heart.

Perhaps after a long, long time——

But she did not want to wait a long, long time—while others, much more sensible and with a better sense of values, tried to interest Giles. She wanted him to know now, *now* that the fever was over, the madness had gone.

That's what it was like, she thought. Like a fever or an obsession or something. And very occasionally—did he know it?—the real, sane me broke through.

Like the time when she had cried suddenly at the thought of having exploited him, or kissed him impulsively in her momentary awareness of his goodness. There had been that moment, too, only a few hours ago, when *he* had kissed *her*, and tugged at her heart-strings so unexpectedly, with his half teasing, half tender injunction to enjoy herself with his rival.

And above all, there had been the passionate instinct for rightness, when she had refused, almost fiercely, to take off his ring.

"That at least I wouldn't do for Paul," she muttered. "Even in my most besotted bewilderment."

But how little those incidents weighed against her foolish determination to keep Giles at a distance. If they had started off differently, she might perhaps have seen more clearly. But she had been scared—she saw that now—by the fact that she was, theoretically, linked with him, and she had instinctively resisted the slightest attempt to give reality to the agitating fantasy they had built up.

It was all wrong from the beginning, she thought sadly. *He* saw the truth of things. But I didn't. Oh, I wish—I wish——

But she hardly knew what she wished, except that

Giles could somehow be there, and she could explain everything, and tell him how dreadfully, dreadfully silly and mistaken she had been.

As it was, she just had to be satisfied that at least she had escaped from that terrible party, without Paul knowing she was there, and she had to be thankful that privacy and seclusion were hers.

But, even as she tried to congratulate herself on these small mercies, it seemed that privacy and seclusion were also to be denied her. For at that moment the bell rang.

Margaret glanced at the clock and wondered indignantly and rather despairingly which of her sister's acquaintances could possibly be calling at this hour. If she had not had the light on, she would just have sat there and let them ring, she thought resentfully. Even as it was——

Then she suddenly realized that, of course, it must be Elinor herself. Unable to blot out sisterly anxiety with present pleasure, the dear girl had evidently decided to cut short her evening too.

It was touchingly good of her—though, to tell the truth, Margaret would still much rather have been left alone. But, in her bruised state, she was grateful for anyone's kindness and concern. And, jumping to her feet, she ran quickly downstairs and threw open the front door.

But it was not Elinor who was standing outside on the step. It was Giles.

"I'm sorry to——" he began. And then, in stupefaction, "*Meg!* But why aren't you at the dance?"

"Oh, Giles——" He was so much like a beloved phantom, miraculously conjured up by her own longing for him, that she could only repeat his name. "Giles—Giles—how did you know?" She caught her breath on a sob. "I wanted you so much. I thought you were miles away. I don't understand——" There was another sob, and she pressed her hand against her lips to keep back yet more.

"Darling, what on earth——?" He was inside the hall

now and his arms were round her. "Don't cry. What is it?"

But she couldn't tell him. She couldn't say anything. The flood of tears which she had been keeping more or less in check for over an hour was suddenly released. She just stood there, shaking her head and weeping.

There was another second of astonished silence. Then, without waiting to ask more questions, Giles pushed the front door shut with his foot, and, picking her up in his arms, he carried her upstairs and into the flat, and set her down in the armchair by the fire.

"I d—didn't know anyone could really d—do that," she said with a gulp. "Outside books, I mean."

"Do what?" He handed her a clean handkerchief, which she gratefully accepted.

"Carry a well—n—nourished girl upstairs." A faint smile struggled across her woebegone, pale face.

"It takes a bit of doing. But opportunity's a fine thing." He stood and grinned down at her. But his eyes were anxious.

"Th—thank you." She handed him back his handkerchief, having done some mopping-up operations. Then she rubbed her hands nervously together and looked away from him into the bright, impersonal glow of the electric fire.

He made no attempt to hurry her. And after a while she said:

"I don't know quite where to begin."

"Shall I begin for you? I suppose that blighter let you down, and started paying court to some other girl?"

"Yes—that, of course." She sounded strangely indifferent, and Giles raised one eyebrow, in the way Penelope admired. "But that doesn't matter now because——"

"Doesn't matter?" He dropped on one knee beside her chair and put his arm round her. "Doesn't matter? Do you realize what you said, my darling?"

She nodded, but she refused to look at him.

"It doesn't matter to you that Paul Freemantle is running after another girl?" He seemed unable to repeat it often enough. "But why, Meg? Why doesn't it matter?"

"Because I don't love him any more," she said slowly. "I don't even love what I thought he was. And I heartily dislike what I find he is."

"And you told him so—and came home from the party?" Giles's handsome eyes sparkled with amused appreciation.

"No, I didn't even bother to tell him so. I just—saw him for what he was, and came home from the party."

"And sat here all by yourself, my poor lonely little Meg? and—*what* was it you said to me when you opened the door?" Suddenly, his vivid face was smiling and radiant. "You said—'How did you know?' and, 'I wanted you so much.' Oh, Meg——" And he put his smiling lips against her cheek and kept them there for quite a long time.

"I must explain——" she whispered.

"There's nothing to explain."

"But there *must* be. How am I to make you believe that—that this isn't just disappointment and pique because of Paul?"

"But I never thought that, darling!"

"D—didn't you?" She timidly put out her hand against his cheek, and he turned his head immediately and kissed the palm of her hand. "Do you mean that you *understand*, without my having to tell you?"

"What do you want me to understand, love?" He smiled at her so reassuringly that she was able to grope for the right words.

"Do you really believe—the truth—that this evening brought a—a sort of revelation, about you, as well as *him*?"

"If you tell me so, I believe it."

"Oh, Giles, is it really as simple as that? You're the most wonderful, understanding, *easy* person in the world. I can't believe all this is happening. I can't even quite understand how it came to happen." She suddenly put her head down against his shoulder, because it seemed the most natural place in the world to put it. "How did you *come* here, to begin with, just as I was so longing for you? It was like a miracle—opening the door and finding you there."

"I'm sorry to have to give a very mundane explanation." He dropped a light kiss on her hair. "I felt a bit restless about going home, so I stayed in town and had some dinner here. Then, when I got back into the car, I realized that you'd dropped your wallet out of your handbag——"

"*Had* I? I never realized—Oh, of course, I wouldn't, because I've been using my evening bag all the time."

"I knew you'd be upset when you discovered the loss, and I remembered that Elinor has a friend living here. So I came by, on the chance of her being here. And when I saw the light, I assumed that she was."

"Oh, Giles, than heaven I wasn't crying in the dark. I nearly did just that! And when I heard your ring at the bell, and thought it was some friend of Elinor's, I wished I *had* been in the dark, because I just wanted to sit here and be miserable, all on my own."

"And then I had to barge in." He sounded amused again.

"Oh, I'm so unspeakably, rapturously glad that you did! I couldn't believe that I'd ever be happy again. I felt sure I'd lost you——"

"You don't lose me so easily," he asserted calmly.

"Don't be so cock-a-hoop about it now," she said, on a note of loving reproach. "As far as you know, *you'd* lost *me*."

"I never really believed that."

"Oh, Giles, you did!" She raised her head and looked at him.

"No," he insisted. "Even in my worst moments, I never really thought Paul would get you."

"But you *must* have!" She was incredulous, but

intrigued. "How could you possibly think anything else?"

"By reminding myself that you and I, whatever our faults and weaknesses, are real people, while he is just a charming, self-confident façade. And real people tend to find each other, in the end. Besides," he added simply, "I loved you, and I meant to have you."

"Oh, darling Giles——" She leaned forward and kissed him—"that's the best, and most illogical reason in the world." And contentedly she put her head down against his shoulder again and stared blissfully into the fire.

Then, after quite a long time, she said dreamily:

"You did think you'd lost me at one time, you know. You practically said so—don't you remember? You said there always has to be a loser in these things."

"I remember." He laughed softly, and put his cheek down against her hair. "I meant it too. And I was right. Because *I* didn't intend to be the loser, darling. I cast that role for Paul Freemantle. And, to my way of thinking, he'll play it to perfection."

GOLDEN HARLEQUIN LIBRARY

Now 24 Volumes!

Harlequin readers will be delighted! We've collected seventy two of your all-time favourite Harlequin Romance novels to present to you in an attractive new way. It's the Golden Harlequin Library.

Each volume contains three complete, unabridged Harlequin Romance novels, most of which have not been available since the original printing. Each volume is exquisitely bound in a fine quality rich gold hardcover with royal blue imprint. And each volume is priced at an unbelievable $1.75. That's right! Handsome, hardcover library editions at the price of paperbacks!

This very special collection of 24 volumes (there'll be more!) of classic Harlequin Romances would be a distinctive addition to your library. And imagine what a delightful gift they'd make for any Harlequin reader!

Start your collection now. See reverse of this page for full details.

H